GENDER IN AMERICA

TWELVE SHORT STORIES

SIMON LENNON

Gender in America: Twelve Short Stories
Fiction (Short Stories, Anthology)
Published by Pine Hill Books
Copyright © 2019 by Simon Lennon
All rights reserved.
ISBN 978-1-925446-32-6 (electronic)
ISBN 978-1-925446-33-3 (paperback)
64,000 words
Cover image: Philadelphia, Halloween, 1998

To my youngest son

CONTENTS

1 TOYS

Old America was a time of comfortable communities and fond families, when adults and children never shied away from the differences between men and women, boys and girls. They played together and apart, more so together at some stages of life and more so apart at others.

Two decades into twenty-first century America, communities and families, in any meaningful sense, had become rare. Those that remained had become small, much smaller than they had been. They offered little to Americans looking to feel parts of something bigger than their individual selves.

To older people who remembered America's past and to anyone else who knew of it, the dwindling reflections of old America became treasured. Those reflections were never more enchanting than in the towns of rural Pennsylvania. With pale brown and orange leaves shining through the dampening air, there was no better time to be in Lahaska, Bucks County than the fall.

At Peddler's Village, windowed dormers protruded from the rooves of buildings, all of them shorter than the trees. It was easy to imagine ghosts quietly looking out, but the clay brick, timber, and stone buildings weren't as old as they appeared to be. That made them better. The charm of life from centuries past wasn't lost for modern amenities, or for being a commercial enterprise.

Wooden boards marked the shops and eating places. Some boards hung ready for the wind, to sway them a little back and forth.

Denzel Derby's store wasn't the only toy store at Peddler's Village, but it may well have been the oldest. Whether it was the best or not wasn't for him to judge, but his wife Florence always thought it was, since before she'd become his wife. It had been his father's store and the only place that Denzel ever worked, but his and Florence's sons and daughters hadn't proceeded into the store as he had done. They had worked there some short times growing up, but they'd all grown older and moved away.

Still, the store remained, Denzel's grandchildren often said, their favorite place to visit and, of course, their favorite toy store. (They had inspected every toy store in Lahaska and in their hometowns, after all, and so they spoke with some authority.) Grandchildren could not visit often enough for doting grandparents like Denzel and Florence.

With their slightly pot bellies, whitening hair, and Denzel with his curly moustache, he and Florence had become much like Denzel's parents had become, decades earlier, before bequeathing the store to them. Far from troubling Denzel, to have become like his father comforted him. Becoming like their parents as they aged once comforted most Americans, but it rarely still did.

Florence always relegated her time in the store to when her motherly and grandmotherly opportunities weren't enticing her elsewhere; she never felt essential to the store as much as she felt essential to her family. Her time at work was fun, to be sure, but fun was never as important to Florence as it was to Denzel. Besides, the store was never so busy as to keep Denzel and Florence from hot chocolate, drunk from the souvenir mugs they'd collected from vacations all around America; they'd never felt a reason to visit other countries.

Back home in the store, a little stress could make Denzel add an extra spoonful of chocolate powder to his mug, or even drink more mugs of hot chocolate than he normally did. Not that the store was every really stressful, but it was his good excuse to take that extra spoonful or fill his mug again.

When their grandchildren visited, Florence dropped a powdery marshmallow or two in their mugs of hot chocolate, while their adult children were known to take marshmallows for their mugs. Between hot chocolates, they, as much as their children, picked away at more marshmallows, popping them surreptitiously in their mouths.

The girls all preferred pink marshmallows. The boys all preferred white ones. Even as adults, the women leant towards the pink and the men away from them, although they were all less demanding if their first choice was inconvenient. No marshmallows remained when they left.

The store was a family business in spirit, if not in legal form, where Denzel and Florence's grandchildren played as if it were their giant nursery. (It essentially was a nursery, as much for adults as for children.) Their sons and daughters, and even their sons- and daughters-in-law, visiting the store, participated. Denzel and his sons and sons-in-law, especially his sons, carried the heavier boxes and items around the store. Florence and her daughters, daughters-in-law, and granddaughters sorted them. With Denzel and Florence otherwise engaged with their grandchildren, any one of them might serve customers.

Never was that spirit more on show than when Denzel and Florence's middle daughter, who'd become quite the artist while tending to her four small children at home in Indiana, painted a picture of her children playing with toys in her parents' Lahaska store. In her painting, as in reality, her two small sons played with Tonka trucks and racing cars. Her two small daughters nursed dolls, brushing their hair.

First seeing the painting unveiled in their home, what had been their children's childhood home, at a special family gathering for Denzel and Florence's fortieth wedding anniversary, they both stood uncharacteristically still. A rare tear fell from Denzel's right eye, as he wrapped his arm around his wife. His artist daughter stepped up to hug both of them. It was a lucky man whose work and family lives had melded as seamlessly as Denzel's had done. That painting of four of his grandchildren, painted by one of his children, assured him that he'd achieved as much success on earth as any man could.

For a long time, the painting remained in Denzel and Florence's home, proudly shown to every visitor. Eventually, when all those visitors had seen it, Denzel realized there was a better place to stand it: a place where dozens, hundreds, and even thousands of people would see it, a place more natural to treasure it even than their home. Thus, late in September, Denzel stood the painting on an easel in the window to his store, facing passers-by browsing from outside. Trucks, dolls, and other toys like those in the picture lay on the shelf and floor below it.

The painting must have stood there for more than a month, attracting only compliments from parents and children seeing it, to the extent any of them remarked upon it, before one little girl, no more than five years of age, stood before Denzel in his store. She was dressed in a dark blue jumper and black slacks. Her dark brown hair might have been short for a girl, but was way too long for a boy. "I think your painting in the window is very mean," she told Denzel, looking up from her low place towards him.

Beside her stood a woman, presumably her mother, looking down at her from above. The woman's face was firm and taut, without even the hint of happiness other adults found inside the store, in the company of their children. Her blue jumper was a slightly paler shade of blue than was her daughter's jumper, but they were pretty much the same. Her black slacks could have been cut from the same cloth as her daughter's had been, in the same style. (Their clothes only made them more alike than they already were.) Her perfectly prepared hair of similar length to her daughter's hair, relative to the sizes of their heads, shone with a monochrome shine. It was probably dyed.

Denzel bent towards the little girl, as far as his back and legs allowed him. "Mean?" he asked. "The painting isn't trying to be mean," he smiled. "It's trying to make you happy."

"I'm not happy," she insisted, becoming even more forthright, looking up at Denzel. "I'm miserable, and it's all because of your painting."

"Why, my little dear?" asked Denzel.

"I don't play with dolls," she told him. "I play with trucks."

"You can still play with trucks," Denzel told her. "You can play with whatever toys you want to play with," he continued, before looking up at her mother still looking down at her, "provided your mother doesn't mind."

The mother turned her eyes to Denzel. "My Madison can play with whatever toys she wants to play with," she told Denzel, as if to say that he should not forget it.

"We have many trucks you can play with," Denzel told Madison, keeping his voice tender as he always did, "yellow ones, red ones, wooden ones, metal ones."

Still bent towards the girl, he looked up and around at the shelves and floor space filled with what seemed an endless array of toys. From close to her child's height, they were even more numerous than they were to adults, standing at adult heights.

Madison persisted. "Why aren't the girls in your painting playing with trucks?" she asked.

Denzel looked back at her. "Those girls are two of my granddaughters," he explained. "They don't play with trucks that I've seen, or that their mother recalled when she painted their picture, I presume, but that doesn't keep you from playing with trucks."

"You shouldn't have pictures like that," Madison told him, never wavering from the conviction in her voice. "You should have boys and girls playing with all the toys."

Denzel stood up to face her mother. Before he could speak, her mother did. "I've raised my child properly," the woman told him. "I've never see paintings like this in Chicago."

"I've not been to Chicago for a long time," said Denzel.

"I've not seen paintings like this anywhere," she told him, "and I've been everywhere."

"My daughter painted this for my wife and me," Denzel explained. "She gave it to us for our fortieth wedding anniversary."

"You should ask her to repaint it," she told him, "or keep it at your home where sensitive children can't see it."

Denzel opened his hands to her. "It is a painting," he said to her, "for children."

"It can be very traumatic for a sensitive girl to see such a painting," the woman told him. "You should have thought of that. Your daughter should have thought of that."

Denzel shook his head, trying to think of something to say. As if it might inspire him, he turned towards the painting, although he couldn't see it very well from inside the store.

"And what about the boys?" the woman asked him. "What are you telling boys who don't want to play with trucks? What are you telling boys who want to play with dolls?"

"I'm not telling them anything," answered Denzel. "It's a painting."

Denzel turned and walked away from them, as he'd never before turned and walked from customers who'd not obviously concluded their conversation with him. There were other customers in the store he could have approached, but the cheerfulness that normally overflowed from him was hard to find. Instead, he stood before the shelves of kits to make balsa wood airplanes, only because nobody else stood near him. On one kit was a picture of a small boy with an airplane he'd supposedly made. Denzel turned the box face down, where nobody saw it.

Madison's voice interrupted his seclusion. "I want you to remove the painting," she told him, looking up from her place standing beside him.

He turned to face her. "No other person has asked me to remove it," Denzel answered her.

"I'm not asking."

Denzel looked back at her mother scrutinizing him. He looked back at Madison. "There are many, many things in this world that I don't like," he told her, "but I can't just go up to people and demand they change."

"I want you to remove the painting," the girl said again.

Denzel walked back towards her mother. Madison walked with him. Before Denzel could say anything, Madison told her mother, in a voice as loud as any in the store, "He won't remove the painting."

The mother looked at Denzel. "Madison wants you to remove the painting," the mother told Denzel.

"Please, Mrs. ..."

"Ms.," she corrected him, "Ketteridge."

Denzel looked at her, her rigid face, her punishing eyes amidst black eyeliner. He looked back at Madison, looking back at him with her mother's eyes. Crouching down, a little closer to her than he normally crouched, he addressed her. "I am sorry, Madison," he told her. "I am sorry if, for all the things for which I'm sure you've asked in your short sensitive life, even demanded, nobody has ever once refused you."

The mother answered for Madison. "You are a rude, mean, little man," she told Denzel.

Standing up to face her, Denzel kept his gentle voice. "I have never entered a shop and demanded the shopkeeper change anything to accommodate me," he told her.

"Don't you ever think of anyone but yourself?"

Denzel looked as much at the girl as the mother. "Can I show you some toys?" he asked them both. "I can show you trucks, and cars, and dolls..."

"Do you listen to anyone but yourself?" Ms. Ketteridge asked Denzel.

He looked around the store, at other parents and children, grandparents perhaps, quietly examining the toys. If they spoke it was only to each other, politely.

"If I can get you anything," Denzel told Ms. Ketteridge and her daughter, "I would be very pleased to do so. If not, then excuse me please. I have other customers."

Denzel left them to approach those customers. Talking with another mother and her young daughter, this little girl holding a doll, Madison interrupted them. "Have you seen the painting in the window?" Madison asked the other little girl. "It's horrible."

The girl looked up at her mother. "Mommy?" she asked.

Madison took the doll from the other girl's hand. She dragged the doll behind her and dropped it to the floor.

Madison's mother was soon there, confronting that girl's mother. "Do you want stores telling you what toys your children must play with?" Ms. Ketteridge asked the girl's mother. "Do you want this man telling you what toys you must buy boys and what toys you must buy girls?"

Denzel answered both mothers, but really the mother whose name he didn't know. "I'm not telling any child what toys he or she must play with," he told them.

The woman looked hurriedly back at Denzel. She looked back at her daughter.

"I'm not telling any parents what toys they must buy their sons or buy their daughters," Denzel continued. "It's just a painting: a nice painting, people say."

The second woman took her daughter by the hand. "We should go," she told her, leading her from the store.

Denzel watched her leave, before tiredly picking up the doll that Madison had dropped on the floor and returning it to a shelf. Looking back around the store, he saw that Madison and her mother had bailed up a couple with two children, looking at some toys.

With Denzel approaching them, but not yet reaching them, the two children put down the toys they'd been holding. The parents began walking to the door.

"May I help you?" asked Denzel.

They didn't answer him. They continued walking from the store.

Denzel turned back to Ms. Ketteridge. "Can't you let the boys be boys and the girls be girls?" he asked her. "Let them like what they like and not like what they don't, whatever you or any painting has to say?"

"You let me raise my child without brainwashing her," demanded Ms. Ketteridge. "You don't have to show that revolting painting."

"You don't have to look at it," said Denzel, constantly finding new expressions he'd never before needed. "You don't have to be in our store."

Through his lifetime in that store, Denzel had never asked anyone to leave. Even when the shop was due to close for the day, he and Florence kept it open until the last customer departed of his or her will.

Madison and her mother didn't leave. Her mother led them to other customers in the store.

Denzel retreated to the counter where he made his sales, although he wasn't certain he would make any more while Madison and her mother remained. Into a small chair behind the counter, Denzel slumped.

Beyond the counter, he heard the commotion of objects moved and falling. Denzel stood up to see Madison's mother standing at the window display, knocking over the easel as she picked up the painting by Denzel's daughter. A customer standing nearby also watched.

Denzel hurried around the counter towards the window, where Ms. Ketteridge held the painting with both her hands, struggling to carry it, her handbag hanging twisted from her shoulder. Her legs and feet had scattered the toys once neatly on the floor.

"This is my shop," Denzel told her, as he'd never before felt the need to tell anyone. "This is my painting."

"This is my child," replied Ms. Ketteridge, holding the painting close to her with the back of the painting visible and her body obscuring the artwork. "I'm keeping this awful painting until you've made your wretched little toyshop suitable for sensitive children."

The door to the shop opened. Denzel turned to see Florence returning; she'd been elsewhere doing something. Her eyes agog, looking around at the mayhem, the door closed behind her. "Denzel?" she asked her husband.

"If this is your husband," Ms. Ketteridge answered Florence, "you should teach him one or two things about equality." Ms. Ketteridge turned back to Denzel. "We are staying at the Golden Plough Inn this evening. In the morning, we will return here. If we find there are no toys designated particularly to boys or girls but are offered to all children, equally, then I will return this appalling painting to you, provided you keep it in whatever creepy little home you occupy."

Denzel wearily shook his head, not refusing her as much as trying to comprehend her. "Why not simply buy your daughter a truck?" he asked her.

"And leave here with you thinking this painting is acceptable? Never!"

Holding the painting against her chest with both her arms, Ms. Ketteridge stormed towards the door, her daughter following. Florence stepped back and out of their way.

"Madison, darling," said Ms. Ketteridge, "the door..."

Her daughter hurried around her to the door, which she opened. Denzel and Florence watched them leave with Denzel and Florence's painting, the door closing behind them.

The customer who'd watched the commotion and must have heard every word in argument, walked quickly to the door. Without facing Denzel or Florence, he opened the door and left. The door closed again.

With only two of them left in the shop, Florence stepped closer to her husband. He told her every detail of his experience with Ms. Ketteridge and her daughter.

"We could call the police," said Florence.

"No, Mother," answered Denzel, shaking his head, as he'd learnt to say in front of their children decades earlier and occasionally said again. "This is still meant to be a toy store: a happy place."

Denzel knelt down on the floor, where he stood neatly upright every doll and toy that Ms. Ketteridge had knocked over. He tidied the shelves so the view from outside through the window was neat again, with even the easel standing properly erect, but without a painting on it.

A woman entered the store, with presumably her daughter. More customers soon followed, some buying things, some not, as happened. A little muted from her normal chirpiness, Florence spoke and smiled with them. She completed their purchases, while Denzel inspected every sign and display in the store, every shelf and space, for anything that suggested boys played with the toys Denzel had only ever seen boys play with, or that girls played with the toys that Denzel had only ever seen girls play with.

Teddy bears were all right. Boys and girls played with teddy bears. Adults bought teddy bears.

Each time Denzel found a colorful cardboard box picturing the toy inside it, with a child of the only gender that he'd seen playing with that toy, or even examining it in the store, Denzel hid the box behind other boxes. Where there were no other boxes to conceal them, he stowed them in a cupboard, to bring out again the next day after Ms. Ketteridge and her daughter left.

As he checked, Denzel mulled over the realization that Ms. Ketteridge and her daughter hadn't bought anything. They'd never appeared like they would buy anything. They'd never looked at any toys, in so far as he had seen, or asked about any toy in particular. Their only interest had been the painting, it seemed. Perhaps they saw it through the window and entered the store because of it, without ever any interest in the trucks or other toys for sale?

There'd never been a government or other inspector as daunting as the one, or two, due to revisit Denzel and Florence's toyshop the next morning. Cleanliness and safety, so immaculate in the store and throughout Peddler's Village, were of no consequence to Ms. Ketteridge. Not only were her rules stricter than other rules governing a toyshop, but she was more zealous than mere government officials in enforcing them.

No number of mugs of hot chocolate or extra spoonsful of chocolate powder calmed Denzel that day. When he had the chance, he slipped away and bought Florence and him a packet of marshmallows. He knew he shouldn't, without their grandchildren visiting, but he felt he needed something sugary to alleviate his thoughts of Ms. Ketteridge.

Without Ms. Ketteridge watching, Florence ate the pink marshmallows. Denzel ate the white ones.

Between the requirements of customers, entering and leaving, Denzel and Florence checked and rechecked every visible corner of the store. They studied every shelf, wall, and floor space for anything Ms. Ketteridge and her daughter might have missed that morning but might detect the next: a picture of a boy with a toy car; an image of a girl with ponytails in her hair. Denzel stood outside to look over the shopfront and timber board inviting shoppers. When he was satisfied that everything would satisfy Ms. Ketteridge and her daughter, he and Florence checked again.

In the morning, instead of their usually slow breakfasts at their kitchen table, Denzel and Florence hurried from their home: Denzel's hair uncombed, the dew still on the grass. He and

Florence arrived early in the store, much earlier than they normally arrived and indeed, much earlier than most keepers arrived at Peddler's Village. Without thought of neatness, cleanliness, or fun, but with thought only of anything that might distinguish boys from girls in any way, Denzel again surveyed his family store. Everything ought to be fine, he thought, but wasn't certain. He rechecked again.

Being there anyway, Denzel opened the store early, releasing the door bolts and turning the small sign to '*Open*.' So early in the day, Peddler's Village was quiet.

Slowly, the morning warmed. Other storekeepers came, customers came. With every opening of their door, Denzel and Florence looked to see if Ms. Ketteridge and her daughter appeared. They didn't.

Before departing the preceding day, they'd not set a time to come and Denzel hadn't thought to ask, although any answer Ms. Ketteridge gave would be unlikely to bind her. Being late, and every minute later in the morning or, Denzel feared, the afternoon, was more time to frighten him.

Without the hostage painting in Ms. Ketteridge's possession, Denzel would gladly have never seen her and her daughter again, as he'd never before thought of even the most difficult customers. Ms. Ketteridge and her daughter hadn't even been customers.

Late in the morning, they finally arrived. Ms. Ketteridge and her daughter again wore blue jumpers almost matching above dark slacks, but different jumpers and slacks to those they'd worn the previous day. In one hand, Ms. Ketteridge carried a large shopping bag from the Pewter Plus store nearby. She and her daughter were not carrying Denzel and Florence's painting.

"Ms. Ketteridge," said Denzel, in the minimum of a greeting, "Madison."

Without a word to Denzel, Florence, or each other, Ms. Ketteridge and her daughter slowly inspected the store. Sometimes, Ms. Ketteridge placed her shopping bag on the floor beside her legs to examine something on a shelf with both her hands. Most of the time, she needed only her eyes; her shopping bag remained in her hand. They checked every image they could as another person might check the shelves for dust; there was no dust in Denzel and Florence's store.

Ms. Ketteridge paused at the shelves of dolls, without

disturbing them. She presumably left them there to be bought for boys, although none would be.

She paused at the shelves of toy cars, trucks, and other vehicles, without disturbing them. Another chance for her to buy a toy truck for her daughter, she passed.

Denzel watched both of them, but more so Ms. Ketteridge. He followed them from a distance, in as much as there could be any distance in his store. Florence tended to the customers and, when customers did not require her, also watched them, but more so Madison.

Any time Ms. Ketteridge or her daughter paused too long anywhere, Denzel's breathing slowed. He tried to study what she studied, searching for what she searched, until she stepped along. Denzel breathed freely again.

When she'd inspected every spot around the store, some spots two or three times, Ms. Ketteridge approached Denzel. Florence approached them, keeping a small distance away. Madison stood beside her mother. "I'll bring you back your painting," Ms. Ketteridge told Denzel, loud enough for Florence to hear. Before Denzel could feel relief, she spoke again. "Whenever I'm near Lahaska, as I am from time to time, I'll pop by to check that everything is in order."

The boxes he'd hidden that morning would come out again that afternoon, thought Denzel. Once sold, he would be reticent to order more.

Ms. Ketteridge continued. "I don't want you slipping back into bad habits," she explained.

"Does your daughter ever not get what she wants?" asked Denzel.

"Madison doesn't tell me what to do," she answered, starting to leave.

"Aren't you going to buy anything?" asked Florence.

"Not from this store."

"Do you have a husband?" Denzel asked her.

She stopped to turn and face him. "Why would I not have a husband?" she demanded of him, without waiting for his reply. "He's at his office in Chicago. I needed time for myself."

"But you took the time to enter our store," remarked Denzel, "to spend this time worrying about the painting, with my wife and me."

"You should be very glad I did," Ms. Ketteridge told him. "You should thank me for helping you."

She turned and left; her daughter with her. The door closed after them.

The comfort that Denzel and Florence's time with her that day and the preceding day would soon end was tempered with the dread for her return, some wintery day. She might not return there until the summer, any summer, but her return would still make that day a wintery day.

The days Ms. Ketteridge would not return would not be as peaceful as all the days once were, for the thought of her peering through the windows and soon barging through the door would always be there. She might come with loud hailers and sirens, kicking down the door, smashing through the window, or she might again walk in as innocently as she'd walked in the previous day, initially unnoticed. The result would be the same.

Ms. Ketteridge might return with her daughter, she might not. Her daughter, who'd not said a word that morning that Denzel heard, was strangely unimportant.

A short time later, Ms. Ketteridge and her daughter in tow returned. Instead of carrying her shopping bag, she carried what was presumably Denzel and Florence's painting, under a white sheet. "I didn't want people seeing it," she explained. "You might return the sheet to the Golden Plough Inn when you're finished."

Denzel reached out his arms to recover his and Florence's painting. Pulling away the sheet so he could again feast his eyes upon the painting, he saw the painting had been slashed into a dozen shreds within its frame. "No!" he gasped. "What have you done?"

Florence took hold of one side of the frame. She burst into tears.

Ms. Ketteridge stood unmoved. "We can't have you subjecting other children to your painting," she told them.

"My daughter's beautiful painting," Denzel panted, shaking his head, still looking at the shreds and whatever slices of imagery survived, "her beautiful children: what will she say? What will they say?"

"Your daughter should have thought of other people when she painted it," insisted Ms. Ketteridge. "She can paint another picture, more sensitively to other people's feelings this time."

Denzel hugged his daughter's painting close to his chest like he was hugging his daughter and her children, comforting them, while Florence held her side of the frame, crying. "What will I tell our children," he asked, without thought as to whether Ms. Ketteridge or her daughter was listening, "our grandchildren?"

Away from the trauma, apparently unaffected by it, Ms. Ketteridge's daughter edged close to a shelf of small dolls. Through his despair, Denzel watched her, drawn to her because of what her mother had done, fearful of what she might do.

Looking momentarily at her mother's back, while her mother faced Denzel and Florence, the little girl raised her right hand to the shelf. With her arms, she might sweep those small dolls to the floor. With her hands, she might carry them to the door and throw them all outside. Nothing she could do to those dolls could matter aside what her mother had already done to Denzel's daughter and grandchildren.

Instead, the little girl slipped a single small doll in her hand. She hid it under her jumper.

She might have taken the doll to keep another girl from playing with it. Denzel couldn't know.

Alternatively, she, Madison, might have taken the doll to play with, hidden less from Denzel and Florence than from her mother. In her bedroom at her home or in a park or other place outside her mother's watch, she might hold it in her hand as if it were her child. She might caress it like a baby, as some girls did with dolls. For that possibility, however massive or miniscule, Denzel said nothing.

Ms. Ketteridge turned around, until she faced her daughter. "Come along, Madison," she said, approaching her daughter stepping back towards her. She took Madison by her hand and turned towards the door outside, her head held high and her long arm dragging her daughter a little higher from the floor behind her, while her daughter's secret doll remained hidden beneath her jumper. "Let's see if there's more respect for people from the bookshop."

2 LADY HOARE

America's first ports were along the Atlantic Ocean, for reasons self-evident to people then. What had been the principal port along that part of the Connecticut colony and state, in Mystic, eventually became best known for its maritime museum, founded in 1929. Resplendent with old ships and exhibiting the life of an old seaport, Mystic Seaport would become the largest maritime museum in the United States. People with little interest in maritime history otherwise couldn't help but find an interest if they lived nearby. Many a traveler found it simply by visiting.

Whenever he knew people planning to stay nearby, Norman Carstairs insisted they stay up the hill in the Inn at Mystic. Ideally, especially if they were a married couple, they'd stay in the Gatehouse, when it was open. Separate from the main hotel building, with its sea views from elegant lounges, the Gatehouse's only attraction might have been that the great actor Humphrey Bogart and rising young actress Lauren Bacall spent their honeymoon there in 1945, but that was enough reason to stay there for Norman and anyone he was able to persuade.

The larger room that charismatic Bogart and beautiful Bacall had occupied was later divided into four smaller rooms, but that probably wasn't so more people could feel they'd slept in Bogey and Bacall's room. If, for any reason, Norman and his wife of more than thirty years ever had to spend a night or two out of their home without leaving Mystic, then they would sleep at the Inn. That Bogart died in 1957 and sultry Bacall remained the loving widow through her subsequent marriage until her death in 2014, only added to the romantic legend.

Through it all, the functions of a town and people continued. Being retired from his vocation and his wife active with her volunteering, Norman had the time and inclination to volunteer for roles he thought important. He thought public libraries, like his private library, were important.

As much for Bogart as for the warmth it provided his thinning scalp, Norman wore a dark fedora hat whenever he left his home. He removed it when he entered private homes and offices or when restaurants and the like asked him to remove it. He also removed it to sit through meetings of the Board of Trustees for the public library, established in 1893, because there felt something personal about them.

He earned no remuneration for being on the Board, not even for being its president. Nobody wanted money wasted on what the trustees gladly gave their time to do; as often as not, they were also donors. If there was any reward beyond Norman's satisfaction for contributing to the library, it was the appreciation that library users conveyed to him, once in a long while. Standing with him in conversation, townspeople might have felt they had no choice but to thank him. Nobody bothered to write letters to him or the other trustees expressing gratitude, but people rarely bothered to write letters to anybody thanking them for anything anymore.

Thus Norman should have known something was amiss when a woman, whose name he could not recall but who nevertheless knew him in his dark fedora hat, came bouncing up to him along the sidewalk on Library Street. "You're supposed to represent our interests," she told him. "The library is a place to bring children."

"I do represent your interests," answered Norman. "My grandchildren are often in the library, quietly."

"Are you going to sit your children in front of Lady Hoare?"

"Who is Lady Hoare?"

"I suggest you find out what's going on in your library!" The woman, who had felt no need to introduce herself, raised her head with a long, high breath and hurried away.

Norman continued the short way to the library, to which he'd been headed anyway. Not only had Norman never before heard of Lady Hoare, he knew of no women who carried the title lady. Several women he knew deserved the title lady. Others thought they deserved the title. He knew of no man or woman with the family name Hoare.

The library was quiet that day, as it always was. A page turning could seem noisy in such serenity, but turning pages were serene as few other sounds could be. A man stepping here, a woman there carrying two books to borrow, made little noise.

Standing at her desk was Miss Dalrymple, not quite thirty years of age. Norman knew the names of most library staff, not merely because he thought he should.

Even the words from Miss Dalrymple behind the desk were hushed, audible to the woman with whom she spoke as they weren't audible to anybody else. If librarians had one skill above all others, it was their voice that reached only as far as the person to whom it was addressed, but no further.

Like any good librarian, Miss Dalrymple could correct an unruly patron as forcibly as anyone, but her words pierced the air with almost pinpoint accuracy towards their target. Not quite being pinpoint accuracy, the waves they spread elsewhere disturbed the still of her public library. Everybody else turned to see the target of her correction, punishing him or her without meaning to do so, before those waves quickly abated and everything fell quiet again. The person she had corrected was particularly quiet thereafter, even if all he or she did was step quickly outside the building to answer the ring of his or her telephone.

Seeing Norman, Miss Dalrymple dipped her head and smiled, silently. He removed his hat from his head, holding it in his hand, as a courtesy to her.

Stepping towards her, Norman saw the small, colorful paper notices at the front of her desk. Norman often checked those notices, and often attended the author talks and other events they advertised, as well as the Shakespeare Club and even the Cribbage Club, but not the Tai Ji Quan. There'd been many events for children as well as adults in the various rooms and spaces of the library building, but never before had Norman seen the notice for a reading of children's books in the Ames Room by Lady Hoare.

Norman picked up a copy of the notice, studying first of all the photograph printed there. Lady Hoare was obviously a man, made up with thick and garish make-up that no woman ever wore. His loud, blazing pink dress demanded to be noticed. His bouffant hair was molded into a show all its own.

Women were beautiful, knew Norman. His wife was beautiful. Miss Dalrymple was beautiful, without a hint of make-up and with no more than a brush through her hair, it seemed. All the female librarians at the Mystic Seaport Library were beautiful, as were the other female staff.

Lady Hoare was not beautiful, nor feminine. He was willfully grotesque: misogynistic as nobody in Connecticut would accept from a man dressed like a man. He reduced women to their clothes, hair, and make-up and then lampooned them for all to see, but planned to read unnamed children's stories to the children at the library on the afternoon of the twenty-eighth that month.

Norman collected all the notices in his free hand, leaving none behind for anyone else to see, before looking back at Miss Dalrymple watching him. "Is Jacqueline in?" he whispered.

Jacqueline Yerbury was the library director. She too was beautiful, thought Norman, although he'd never say so. He never said any women were beautiful, except his wife and daughters.

Miss Dalrymple whispered in reply. "I'll let her know you're here, Mister Carstairs."

With his hat in his hand, Norman waited. Miss Dalrymple stepped away, softly tapped on a closed door, opened it, and stepped inside. Soon appearing at her open office door was Jacqueline, a sprightly woman of thirty something with flowing auburn hair quite unlike that of any other librarian there. She'd managed a bookstore in Vermont before moving with her young family to Mystic.

She and Norman approached each other. "Can we please speak privately, Jacqueline?" whispered Norman.

For the first time not just since Jacqueline's appointment but for the first time altogether, Norman entered the library director's office. Never before had he personally intervened in a matter in the library, raising an issue with the director away from meetings of the Board of Trustees and resolutions carrying the Board's authority, but Norman had never before seen anything like the notice for Lady Hoare.

Jacqueline closed her office door. Norman remained standing in front of her, offering her the notices he'd taken from the public desk.

She took the notices in her hand. She needed only to glance at them to know what they were.

"We can't have people like that reading books to children," Norman told her, a little quieter than he normally spoke even in that closed office, because the office was in the library. "I'm not sure we can have people like that reading books to adults."

Jacqueline walked away from him around her desk, behind which she sat. If she did so to cause Norman to sit in the chair facing her, then she succeeded; Norman was much too much the gentleman to remain standing when a woman sat.

Norman sat with his hat on his lap. "I don't want pictures spreading around the country of impressionable children in our library," he told Jacqueline, "looking trustingly up from the floor at Lady Hoare. When people think of Mystic, Connecticut, I want them to think of sailing ships, scenery, and family vacations, along with films and pizza, not transvestites mingling with children."

"I want people to think of a welcoming community."

"They do that now."

"They're wrong, if your attitude to Lady Hoare is anything to go by."

Norman might have expected more courtesy from the library director to the president of the Board of Trustees, but he'd never before had a conversation like this one with Jacqueline Yerbury. "He'd be welcome here if he dressed like a man and behaved like a man," said Norman, "but he doesn't want that anonymity."

"He, or she, has the right to dress as he or she wants," protested Jacqueline.

"We have the right to insist anyone entering our library dress in a manner becoming of this community," retorted Norman, "and becoming of his or her gender."

"Lady Hoare is a character, part of a show, in New Haven," explained Jacqueline.

New Haven had declined a lot, thought Norman. Most of America had.

"I've not seen the show," continued Jacqueline, "but that's nothing to do with her offer to visit us."

"I hope he doesn't involve children in his show," said Norman. "New Haven used to be so nice."

"I don't know whether he wants us to call him a man or she wants us to call her a woman," insisted Jacqueline, "but we can't assume anything about the person behind the act."

"What books will he read?" asked Norman. "Will they be fictitious fables that people aren't of the gender they're biologically born to be, or aren't naturally attracted to people of the other gender?"

"I can select the books."

"Can we select his clothes, shoes, and hairstyle?" asked Norman. "Can we prohibit him from wearing make-up? Can we insist he be honest about the gender he purports to be?"

"Only she can do that." Jacqueline insisted. "Only I can do that for me. Only you can do that for you."

"You and I aren't pretending to be what we're not," said Norman. "We're not confusing people, least of all children. We're not ridiculing the gender we're not."

The two remained sitting in their chairs, facing each other. Jacqueline's authority over the library was no less plain than was Norman's lack of authority over her, sitting there alone. Norman was strangely ineffective for the president of trustees in his dealings with the director of the library, as he'd never felt at the meetings of trustees, with Jacqueline there. Those meetings had never discussed restricting anyone from using any of the rooms.

"I must be free to manage this library as I see fit," Jacqueline told him.

Her reports and meetings with trustees were primarily concerned with budgets and fund raising. If they mentioned anything unusual, it was typically to excite trustees about the good things happening at the library, without thought that trustees might approve or disapprove of them. If any trustees had not approved, they'd never expressed disapproval, during Norman's time among them.

Norman's only concern had been the twelve weekly sessions of Tai Ji Quan because he thought martial arts weren't proper offerings for a Connecticut public library, but the other trustees had been unconcerned. The president had no greater vote than other trustees had, except as a casting vote in the event of a tie, but he'd been the only trustee to express a reservation.

That might have been the only time through Norman's tenure as a trustee that trustees had not shared a unanimous consensus, but Norman was not the president simply because he agreed with other trustees all the time. He was the largest donor offering to be president.

"The trustees," Norman told Jacqueline, "are responsible for ensuring community standards are maintained within this library."

"Have you spoken with the other trustees?" asked Jacqueline, with a confidence in those trustees' attitude Norman feared was well-founded.

The dozen library trustees were theoretically chosen with a thought to the diversity of experience they brought to the Board. In practice, they were the residents of Mystic, Noank, and the surrounding areas who cared enough about the library to give up their time for a three-year term. By chance and character, as much as by the range of experience among those residents, it all worked very well.

Norman would call the trustees together for a special meeting two nights later to discuss Lady Hoare's offer to visit the library. In the interim, Jacqueline would consult with library staff. There would be no more notices for Lady Hoare in the library until after the trustees' meeting.

Thursday evening, nine of the twelve trustees met with Jacqueline in their usual meeting room in the library building: the Ames Room, where Lady Hoare was scheduled to visit. The room was large and bland in its modernity, unlike the old beauty of the building, from the time before functionality had become all-important. Norman sat with his fedora hat resting close to him on the table.

Much like Norman's conversation with Jacqueline in her closed office, trustees spoke at meetings in voices a little quieter than they spoke in other places. They did so simply because they were in the library building, albeit behind closed doors, and perhaps because they were discussing a library.

Each of them sat around the table with a copy of the notice for Lady Hoare in front of him or her. One trustee who'd seen the notices in the library before Norman removed them had felt uncomfortable about it and planned to mention it at the next trustee meeting. Another hadn't been perturbed.

"Hoare?" asked one trustee. "Do we know of anyone named Hoare? Is that really his name?"

"Don't spell it," another trustee responded. "Pronounce it."

The first trustee sat quietly before nodding, eyes wide opened with the sight of recognition. "Oh," she said.

"As women," Norman addressed the five female trustees present, "don't you feel insulted by the misogyny of his make-up and manner? He's insulting the women of the town."

"He's not insulting me," answered one, Margeaux, a large woman of the age of Norman's children, whose only work outside her family home was being a trustee of the library. "Your grandchildren can remain at home."

"I don't want my children feeling they need to ban my grandchildren from the library," said Norman, "not even for an afternoon."

Jacqueline normally refrained from joining discussions between trustees, unless she was specifically invited to contribute. If she spoke, then it was normally after the meeting reached a decision, which she supported.

Norman continued. "A hundred parents will stand outside the library protesting Lady Hoare's presence," he said.

"A hundred isn't many," responded Margeaux, "with the tens of thousands of parents we serve." Margeaux, a mother of two, was rarely as engaged in a Board discussion as she was engaged that evening.

"Among people who don't protest," said Norman, "a dozen would be a lot. Do you want images of them protesting on the evening news?"

"That isn't a reason to cancel Lady Hoare's visit."

Several trustees nodded. None disagreed.

"We could ask Lady Hoare if he thinks it's a reason," replied Norman.

"She might like the publicity."

Another trustee spoke up. "We could poll the parents," he suggested.

Margeaux responded. "Even if every parent but one opposed Lady Hoare coming, and I know that not every parent but one would oppose it, why deny that one parent and that parent's child this opportunity?"

Norman answered her. "Would you want your children sitting close to Lady Hoare?"

"That will be my decision to make," replied Margeaux, before adding as if it had been an afterthought, "along with my husband."

Norman looked around at the other trustees. "What if you safeguard your children, but another child from the school is not so guarded?" he asked them. "What if that child tells your children about the woman who isn't a woman, the man who isn't acting like a man, the man who mocks their mothers? Do you want them confused?"

"I want my children tolerant," responded Margeaux.

"I want my grandchildren secure," retorted Norman.

Margeaux looked around the room. "Don't we want people to read books to our children?" she asked her fellow trustees.

Norman answered her. "If there's no other person willing to

read books to children the afternoon the library scheduled Lady Hoare to come," he said, "then I'll read them books."

Margeaux looked back at him. "Can you read?" she asked. A couple of trustees smiled.

"I've got nothing against Lady Hoare, you understand," said Wilbur, "but could this affect donations to the library?" Wilbur had a particular interest in financial matters for the library exceeding that of most trustees. "Might the town governments supporting us take a dim view?" The library depended not just upon local donors but upon the generosity of the Groton and Stonington town governments.

The meeting was quiet. The enthusiasm with which trustees talked of money coming to the library matched their trepidation at the risk it wouldn't come.

Withholding donations from the library could seem like a threat, but there was little point in donating money without the knowledge of it being used for something good. "If Lady Hoare reads books to children in this library," said Norman, before holding up a copy of the notice, "dressed like he is dressed in this picture, then I will cease my donations to the library."

"Phew," said Wilbur, leaning back in his chair.

"This town will know I have ceased donating money and my reason," continued Norman. "I would assume other donors will do the same."

Margeaux answered him. "The rest of us could raise money from donors around the country wanting Lady Hoare to come," she said. "They'd pour in more money than you and other departing donors do."

Norman nodded. "You could," he said, "but those donors won't give us money for the rest of our library services. We'd become the library for Lady Hoare and people like him reading books to children, but little else."

"We'd remain my library," declared Margeaux.

Norman looked around the room. Nobody else spoke. As president of trustees, Norman put the motion to the meeting to withdraw from Lady Hoare the opportunity to read to children. By the gentle raising of trustee hands for the motion and gentle raising of other hands against it, without abstentions, the vote was tied four each. Jacqueline, the only person paid to be there, had no right to vote.

Trustees murmured, moving around uncomfortably in their chairs. For the first time, Norman prepared to exercise his casting vote. It might have been the first time any president had exercised a casting vote at a meeting of the Board.

Before Norman could do so, Jacqueline spoke up. "If you cast your vote to carry this motion," she asked him, as she must have known he would, "will you tell Lady Hoare that she's not welcome?"

He smiled. "I'll be happy to do so," he told her. "I'd like to talk some sense into him, and if he's willing to come along in men's clothes, without make-up, with his hair combed neatly, behaving like a man, then I'll assume the Board will want to let him read books to children."

"Does he have to wear a fedora?" asked Jacqueline, before looking around the room. "I have spoken with my staff," she told all trustees, as much as she told Norman. Her voice was less threatening than were her words. "If my staff and I cannot decide who comes to this library, then we will withdraw our services."

Trustees moved back in their chairs, but not Norman. "Will you resign?" he asked her.

She looked back at Norman. "We will take strike action."

"Librarians don't strike."

"Trustees don't tell librarians who can read books to children in their libraries."

Norman disagreed with her, but the motion before the Board would be the means to say so. His casting vote would be his answer. "Would you deny people their library because of Lady Hoare?" asked Norman.

"Would you?"

"Yes."

"So would we," answered Jacqueline. "Some things are more important than libraries: values."

"Our children are more important than both," Norman declared. "The town governments supporting us might be quite happy to spare giving us money while we're not paying people wages. They have other demands upon their funds."

"We'll continue working," replied Jacqueline. (The librarians wanted to be paid, thought Norman.) "We will cease collecting fines for overdue books."

Such dereliction of duty might be grounds for dismissal, but

Norman wasn't looking to dismiss anyone, except Lady Hoare. "Refusing to collect fines will leave us with less money to buy books," he told Jacqueline.

"You'll have to let Lady Hoare visit."

"You'll have to stop buying books."

Jacqueline shook her head. She looked at Margeaux, before looking around the room. "The trustees should understand that if they vote to cancel Lady Hoare's visit," she told them, "then the staff will want us to close the library rather than carry out that order. We'll work inside the building on administrative matters, but the doors from the street will remain shut."

Nobody answered. The trustees had their final chance to speak, but didn't.

Norman's eyes moved slowly around the room, dwelling upon each trustee in turn, but a little less time upon Margeaux than upon every other trustee there. He wouldn't ask the trustees if they wanted to change the votes they'd cast, denying Norman his casting vote. The time he spent looking around at them was time enough for them to do so.

None did. Surely, they knew the vote that he would cast.

The vote of the many had become the vote of the one. Exercising his presidential casting vote, Norman carried the motion.

Jacqueline stood up from her chair. "The library will be closed indefinitely," she said. "I don't wish to publicize the reason; I don't wish to embarrass Lady Hoare, or embarrass this Board." She left the room.

Margeaux stood silently, as did the three other trustees who'd voted as she voted to let Lady Hoare visit. They left the room.

The remaining five trustees looked at each other. "My friends," said Norman, with no sense of comfort in the term. "I wish it didn't have to be like this."

There would have been something very sad about seeing the library closed when it ordinarily would have been open. Thus, in the morning, Norman did not approach it. He had no reason to be there anyway, except to ask Jacqueline for the telephone number to call Lady Hoare. That could wait until later in the day.

A soft knock came through the front door of his home. His head bare, Norman answered it, to see a little girl with sweet blonde hair who lived next door, looking up at him.

Norman smiled. There had been a time he would have squatted down to meet her eye to eye, but he'd become too old for that. "Good morning, Ivy," he smiled again.

"Why is the library closed?" Ivy asked him. Ivy's parents and so Ivy knew of Norman's role at the library.

"I am sorry, Ivy," Norman smiled again. "I wish it was open, but we're having a little problem at the moment."

"Can't you fix it?" she asked him. "Can't old people fix everything?"

Again, Norman smiled. "I wish we could," he told her, "but we don't seem able to fix much anymore."

"Please," said Ivy, "I'm sure you can. My grandparents fix everything."

"I'm trying to help you and the other children," he explained. "I'm trying to protect you."

"Please," persisted Ivy, "please, for me."

Norman continued looking at her. If serving her a plate of cookies and glass of milk would make everything all right, then he would, but it wouldn't make everything all right. Instead, he thought again, of all that had been said the previous evening and what more could have been said. "I will see what I can do," he told her, with no idea of what that might be, "I promise."

She smiled. "Oh good," she said. "I know that if you promise something then you'll do it. Other people don't, but you do. My grandparents do, too. Thank you."

Norman watched her leave, walking back along the front path from his and his wife's home. The burden upon his shoulders had never been greater: to give a small girl what she wanted but also to protect her from confusions she was too young to dismiss. Without knowing what to say, Norman telephoned Jacqueline Yerbury inviting them to meet, away from the library.

She said she'd planned to telephone him. She would have made the same invitation.

Norman found Jacqueline where she said she'd be: beside the replica lighthouse along a wharf at the old Mystic Seaport. (Membership of the museum gave them free admission.) The weather was bleak and not one for walking in the Mystic River air, without good reason to be there, but the past let people forget the problems of the present. The sea breeze blustered through the old wooden ships as if the wooden ships weren't there, but every

Mystic resident knew they were.

With thick coats around them and hats on both their heads, Norman and Jacqueline could have been almost indistinguishable to anyone seeing them from a distance. "I wanted to see you where we can talk," she told him, as they started to walk together, "but if we fail to resolve anything, then nobody at the library need know we talked. I've never seen Miss Dalrymple as upset as she is upset today; I've never seen her upset in the slightest, before today."

"My fellow trustees will be pleased to know we talked," said Norman, as they walked.

"Yours is still the casting vote," said Jacqueline. "I know children mean more to you than the library, but the library is still important to you."

"The children I care so much about," said Norman, "include yours."

"I spoke with Lady Hoare," said Jacqueline. "I asked if he could come dressed as a man to read the stories to the children, but he insisted he is Lady Hoare and as Lady Hoare we'd accepted his offer to come."

"Does he know he's a man?" asked Norman.

"I think so," she answered. "I'm not sure. He might not."

Jacqueline stopped walking. She and Norman stood facing each other.

"I don't want to refuse Lady Hoare's offer," she told him, "having accepted it."

Norman waited for her to say something more. Her silence was his invitation to ask for anything else. "Would you remove all notices of the event?" he asked her, thinking aloud as he probably should have mentioned. "Would you withhold all pictures of Lady Hoare and all other mention of the event? Would you hurry him to and from the meeting room so people needn't unnecessarily see him? Will you keep the doors around him closed, so people outside the room needn't hear him; I can't imagine the voice he'll use."

"Children will already know he's coming if they have already seen the notice," Jacqueline pointed out, "or hear about it from someone else who saw it, or see him coming that afternoon."

"There should be other adults in the room with him and the children," said Norman.

"I will be there," Jacqueline told him. "You too can be there."

Norman shook his head, smiling a little at himself. "I'd rather not," he said, "but I'll be satisfied if you're there, watching him, or if Miss Dalrymple is there, watching him."

"Miss Dalrymple won't want to leave her desk."

Norman nodded. Jacqueline smiled. They returned to warmer places. The library doors soon reopened, without a word said about the late opening that day.

Ivy never thanked Norman for what he'd done, but that was fine. Her parents never mentioned it to him or to his wife.

Miss Dalrymple never mentioned anything to him. No librarian did, not even Jacqueline at the next meeting of the Board of Trustees, when Norman briefly reported to Trustees his agreement with Jacqueline, before proceeding to customary matters.

The day of Lady Hoare's visit came. Norman wasn't at the library to see him, but heard later there were no protestors. Nobody seemed to have expected him.

Among the trustees, Margeaux had said she planned to take her children to hear Lady Hoare, but something else came up involving her children. She attended that.

Jacqueline later told Norman about the visit. She had arranged the chairs and tables in the Ames Meeting Room for Lady Hoare to sit facing the wide carpeted floor, on which lay several cushions. In his complete Lady Hoare persona, with its garish make-up, flaming pink dress, and bouffant hair, the still unnamed actor swanned into the library. "I'm Lady Hoare!" he declared.

"Shush!" Miss Dalrymple told him, in her ordinary women's wear, with her modest make-up, patterned dress, and hair unceremoniously neat.

"So sorry, darlings!"

Every swing of his hands and throw of his head was exaggerated, as Jacqueline led him floating to the Ames Room. Soon he sat in his designated chair, holding a book at the ready: *The Wizard of Oz*. Other books that Jacqueline had selected, along with several books that Lady Hoare had brought along that Norman would not have found acceptable, lay on the table beside him.

Near him were several more chairs, from which adults could sit watching the children. In one sat Jacqueline.

The floor could have accommodated several dozen children sitting quietly, listening to him reading. At the time scheduled for the reading to start, none had come.

Jacqueline and Lady Hoare sat there, waiting, with the only

conversation from Jacqueline. "Is Lady Hoare your only role?" she inquired.

Lady Hoare answered in character, with a little of the flamboyance with which he'd arrived. "Is...whatever your name is, yours?"

Jacqueline tried again. "What do you do in your spare time?"

"Be fabulous."

Again, Jacqueline tried. "What do you want from your life?"

"To be even more fabulous."

Their words soon became tedious. It had always been pointless; Lady Hoare wasn't interested in conversation with a woman. The few words he spoke were all in character, playing like lines long repeated from a play never ending.

Describing their would-be conversation later to Norman, Jacqueline would say she tried to find a person behind the persona, but couldn't. She didn't think anyone was there.

Half an hour after the time scheduled for him to start reading, without any children having come, Lady Hoare collected his books to leave. Floating back through the main part of the library, with all the same flamboyant gestures with which he'd arrived, he cried out, "Bye darlings!"

Miss Dalrymple responded: "Shush!"

3 BOY SCOUTS

Through the time of old America, morality expressed people's love and support for each other. They were social norms and mores accepted throughout families and communities because they were families and communities. They safeguarded the very nature of families: men married to women and staying married to raise the children they made together, upon which the communities and their futures depended. Morality especially protected those children for being the most vulnerable among them. All the children among their communities were their children, to nurture for life in their communities or others like them.

Two decades into twenty-first century America, morality had become personal and private: something for people each to decide for themselves and keep to themselves, without it affecting their dealings with others. Those others, in turn, kept their moralities, whatever they each decided they'd be, to themselves. Any particular moralities certainly weren't a matter for laws or the rules of clubs and associations. Morality was thus obsolete, as was no less evident among the Boy Scouts of America than anywhere else.

With its camps, hikes, and other outdoor activities, Boy Scouts had been part of American life since 1910. Boys wanting to experience the open air could always do so alone, but those wanting to do so in a group, or boys whose parents wanted them to do so in a group, became Scouts. Older girls could join the older boys in Venturing and Sea Scouting and, from 2018 and 2019, younger girls could join younger boys as Cub Scouts and Scouts. In its origins, Boy Scouts of America was quintessentially a pack organization, not maintained for people indifferent to others.

It remained so through the rural reaches of Washington State and nowhere more so than Whidbey Island, so far as Henry (known to everyone as Hank) and Abi Goodmas were concerned. More than a few people remarked that Hank must be a Scoutmaster because he wore a thickish brown beard, before Hank corrected them that few Scoutmasters he knew and none of the

Scout mistresses wore beards.

He and Abi were parents to two boys in the Langley Central Scouts troop, Troop 21, where all the Scoutmasters and mistresses were parents to children in the troop. Indeed, if he'd thought about it, Hank would have said that all the Scoutmasters and mistresses he knew from his and other troops were parents to children in their troops, aside from one Scoutmaster who'd enjoyed it all so much that he remained a leader after his three sons grew up and out of Scouts, and even away from Whidbey Island altogether.

Unlike the Scout leaders who'd been roped into their roles because of their children, with varying degrees of effort from existing leaders, one potential new Scoutmaster first appeared as an inquiry through Hank's computer. Lesley Xute wrote that he'd been a Scout leader in Portland, before recently moving to Whidbey Island to work with a small shipyard. Hank presumed he must have children to want to be a Scoutmaster; troops didn't need children as much as they needed leaders, but every new child coming was more comfort that Troop 21 would continue after Hank's sons moved along.

The potential new Scoutmaster would need more words of introduction about Langley Central Scouts than other Scoutmasters had, not having been a parent, but Hank liked telling people about Scouts with far less reason to know than Lesley Xute would have. Hank's introduction to Lesley Xute would be something like the one he gave new parents of boys and girls looking to join, although Lesley's time leading Scouts in Oregon should mean he was already well informed about Scouts in general. If other Scoutmasters and mistresses weren't already friends to Hank and Abi by the time they were inducted, they became friends through the many meetings, camps, and other Scouts activities.

Hank thus had several reasons to invite the potential new Scoutmaster to his family home: an elegant two-story white home behind a white picket fence along Cascade Avenue. (Hank and Abi had done rather well in life, he often thought, without saying so to anyone but Abi.) On the living room wall was a large moose head and antlers: a hunter's trophy, but not from Hank's hunting. It had hung from a wall in a Scout hall, but the church that hosted Langley Central Scouts didn't want it hanging from its walls. None of the other leaders wanted it, some of them because they already had hunters' trophies: their own, their father's, or their grandfather's.

For an interview for a potential new Scout leader, Hank needed only dress as he dressed any evening at home, in a thick woolen shirt and jeans he'd bought from the same sportsmen shop from which he bought all his clothes. (The only shirts that lasted were those from sportsmen shops.) If Hank's time with Lesley Xute, that Monday evening late in fall, was to be a job interview, then it was for a job paying no money and without career paths on offer.

Hank suggested to his sons they meet the potential new leader when he came to their home, but they preferred to play computer games in the den. They'd meet Lesley at the Scouts meeting on Wednesday night, they all presumed. None of them imagined Hank not welcoming a new leader.

Upon hearing the knock from the front door to his home, perhaps softer than other knocks, Hank opened the front door. Lesley's age was indeterminate, with his jet-black, thinly cut hair and slightly pocked complexion, but Hank was most surprised to see that Lesley was so short. Hank was not particularly tall, but Lesley was particularly short. He was shorter than Hank's wife Abi and shorter than their sons.

Lesley dressed much as Hank dressed, but his cotton shirt was brighter and jeans much less worn. (They'd plainly not been bought from a sportsmen shop.) His eyes gazing past Hank, he stepped past Hank into the living room, across the rug. Drawing him as it drew many visitors to Hank's home, and Hank's home hosted a lot of visitors, was the moose head.

His head and neck becoming more arched, Lesley looked up at the moose head high on the wall. Finally, he stood before and beneath it.

"They are beautiful beasts," said Hank. "I only hunt ducks."

Lesley visibly shivered. "I don't hunt," he said.

"Neither does my wife," said Hank, "but she does cook the ducks I bring home."

Lesley turned to him. "You could eat something else?"

Hank shook his head. "Wild duck tastes better than butcher's duck."

"I was thinking more of vegetables."

Abi brought them both mugs of warm tea and a plate of chocolate chip and pecan cookies she'd made that afternoon. She then returned elsewhere in the house; Scouting was more for Hank than for Abi, although it was most of all for their sons.

Hank and Lesley sat in two armchairs facing each other in the living room, holding their mugs of tea. Lesley held his cookie in his hand. Hank had already consumed his.

"What's your line of work, Lesley?" asked Hank.

"Business strategy," answered Lesley, looking around the house, his cookie still uneaten in his hand.

Hank nodded. He didn't really understand what business strategy meant. "I'm a builder," he said, as if theirs were a conversation. "What children do you have?"

Lesley continued looking around the room as he answered, pausing at the sight of the moose head. "I don't have any children."

"None at all?" checked Hank.

Looking back at Hank, Lesley smiled. "I don't have to be a parent to be a Scout leader," he answered.

"Are you married?" Hank asked him.

Lesley shook his head. He looked around the room again.

Being unmarried and childless would have been no surprise in a young man, but Lesley's age so indeterminate had become important. "Do you mind me asking how old you are?" asked Hank.

"I'm forty-three."

Lesley's voice was a little soft, realized Hank, thinking about it. He was clean-shaven, but that didn't mean anything. Concentrating his sense of smell, Hank could not discern a fragrance coming from him, but they were sitting yards apart. "Do you want to get married?" Hank asked him.

Lesley looked back at him. "To you?" he asked.

With Hank's back against the armchair, he would have thought he had no scope for jarring back, but he jarred back. "To a woman," Hank answered, surprised that Lesley had been so foolish to ask the question and that he had been so foolish to feel a need to answer it. "Do you have a girlfriend?" asked Hank. "Have you ever had a girlfriend?"

Lesley remained calm. If Hank's questions had been interrogatory, they'd not obviously bothered him. "You're more interested in me not being married," answered Lesley, "to a woman, than in me not being a parent."

Hank might not have invited Lesley to his home had he known what he suspected about Lesley. Nor would he have met him in a restaurant like the one his home had been, before he bought it. He might have met him at the Scout hall, or he might have not met him at all.

"You must have children, then," said Lesley. "Can I meet them?"

"They're occupied."

"Do you think I harbor unnatural feelings towards children?" asked Lesley, taking a small bite from his cookie.

Lesley's language about such matters was more abrupt than any to which Hank was accustomed. Such feelings hadn't been Hank's contemplation because he never contemplated them in anyone, but Lesley made him think he should. The possibility of them in Lesley's strange and distant mind was another reason to refuse him. It was not the only one. "No," answered Hank, "I don't think that, but I'm not certain that you don't."

"I don't harbor those feelings," insisted Lesley. "I passed the criminal background check in Oregon. I completed the Youth Protection Training. You've got no reason to refuse me."

Hank was unperturbed. "The Mission of the Scouts is supposed to be helping the boys and girls to make ethical and moral choices."

"The Boy Scouts of America has no ethical or moral objection to me being a leader," responded Lesley.

"I object."

"Why?" asked Lesley. "Would you allow me to be a Scout leader if I were married, to a woman? Would you allow me to be a leader if I had children? Are you aware of the Scouting Non-Discrimination Policy?"

"I need to be satisfied that you're someone I want around my sons," said Hank, "and someone I want around other boys and girls on Whidbey Island."

"Let the boys and girls decide whether I can lead them."

"I decide," insisted Hank. "The leaders decide."

The telephone rang on a table. Hank let it ring, although Lesley glanced at it. The ringing stopped; Hank's wife had answered it elsewhere in the house.

Lesley was next to speak. "I know you meet at the Island Church at seven p.m. each Wednesday," he told Hank. "Are you meeting this Wednesday? I can come, introduce myself, and let the boys and girls decide."

"I don't want you coming to our meetings."

"This is America," said Lesley. "You can't stop me."

"This is Langley Central Scouts. I can stop you."

"Let me come to the next meeting, Hank, and if the boys and girls and other leaders decide they don't want me, then you will never see or hear of me again, unless you share an activity with the troop that accepts me as a leader."

"Why not go to that troop now?"

"I'm here, and I think that when you all spend time with me, you'll know what an asset I will be."

"No, Lesley, no."

Lesley fell silent. The mug of tea in his hand, he had barely touched. Hank had barely touched his since he began learning about Lesley, but that was a moment for him to take a mouthful. The tea had cooled.

Again, Lesley was next to speak. "I think you're falling foul of the Scouting Non-Discrimination Policy," he told Hank. "I think you're discriminating against me."

Hank shrugged his shoulders. "I don't think there's anything more for us to say," he told Lesley.

"There's a lot for us to say," insisted Lesley, "but you're not going to say it and there's no point in me saying it, not to you."

Lesley stood up and placed his mug on the wooden coffee table. Hank stood up and stepped across the rug to it, placing Lesley's cup on a coaster so it did not leave a ring on the wood; his wife would have done the same if she'd been there.

In Lesley's hand was the cookie he'd only started to eat. Holding it up, he asked Hank, "May I finish my cookie?"

The question had been facetious. "Go ahead." If Lesley didn't finish eating it, Hank would throw it in the trash after he'd gone.

Lesley took another bite from the cookie. Hank watched him eat, still not finishing it. Never before had Hank watched a person eat a cookie as slowly as Lesley ate that cookie. Never before had he watched any person eating a cookie. Eventually, Lesley finished eating.

"Good night, Lesley," said Hank.

"I'm sorry I haven't met your children."

"I'm not."

Lesley looked back into the house, turning towards the moose head before turning back again. "Tell them I said 'hi'," he told

Hank. "Thank your wife for the hospitality."

Hank saw him to the door. After he'd gone, he found Abi in their bedroom.

"How was he?" Abi asked her husband.

"He isn't suitable," Hank told her, intending not to mention Lesley Xute again. "I wouldn't have imagined being so glad our boys spent a night playing idiot computer games as I'm glad of it tonight."

When next Hank saw their sons, they didn't mention their father's visitor. If they expected to see him that Wednesday evening at the Scout meeting with their father, they didn't mention it.

Hank had thought that would be the end of his dealings with Lesley Xute, until about ten o'clock the next morning. He took a call on his cell phone from Wally Bowden of the Boy Scouts of America, in Seattle. "Yes," Hank had met Lesley Xute. "No," he didn't want Lesley to be a Scoutmaster at Langley Central. "Yes," he was familiar with the Boy Scouts of America's Non-Discrimination Policy. "No," he wasn't going to change his decision.

That conversation having occurred, Hank knew that it was unlikely to be the end of the matter. Within the hour, Wally Bowden called back again. Lesley Xute had engaged legal counsel to advise him of his options, but agreed to meet again with Hank if Wally Bowden was there, that evening.

"Not at my house," insisted Hank. "We don't have use of the Scout hall tonight." More telephone calls later, they agreed to gather at eight o'clock in the meeting room at the Saratoga Inn, along Cascade Avenue from Hank's home.

When he could defer their conversation no longer, after the dinner she had made and in the lounge room of their home, Hank told Abi that Boy Scouts of America required him to meet again with Lesley Xute that evening. "Why, Hank?" she asked him. "Why isn't Lesley Xute suitable to be a Scoutmaster?"

"I like to give people the benefit of the doubt," replied Hank, "but not when doubt puts children at risk." He grappled for words to use, to talk of something never mentioned among ordinary people, least of all to women and the least of the least of all by men to their wives. "He's not normal," said Hank. "He's the sort of man I never thought I'd see in Langley: a man not quite a man, a man but not a man inside. He's not right in the head."

When she'd studied his eyes long enough, Abi left him alone. She seemed to understand.

Donning a hunting jacket, because all his jackets were hunting jackets or Scouts jackets and he didn't want to wear a Scouts jacket, Hank was nonchalantly late to the Saratoga Inn; never before had that big pretty inn been uninviting. Wally Bowden, a burly man, sat to one side of the wooden table in the meeting room. Lesley Xute sat beside him, as if Hank was supposed to see the two of them as a team. Hank knew Wally well enough to know that he and Lesley Xute were not a team.

"I don't want to be here, people," Wally told them, "not in these circumstances."

Hank answered him. "You and I can head back to our place for some tea."

"Not yet," interjected Lesley. "Do you want to solve our little problem, Hank, or don't you?"

"I don't have a problem," insisted Hank.

Wally interrupted them; the meeting was his anyway. "Law suits are a problem, Hank," he told him. "We're going to resolve this tonight, or I believe Lesley when he tells me a judge will resolve it for us."

"We're not going to be persecuted anymore," Lesley told Hank.

"When were you ever persecuted?" Hank asked him. "Not just for the children do I believe you shouldn't be a Scoutmaster, but for you."

"Hank," Wally again interjected. "Lesley." He gave them both moments not to answer, before pointedly facing Hank. "Lesley has proposed that we let the boys and girls of Langley Central decide whether they want him to be a leader. If we do that, then he won't sue Boy Scouts of America and he won't sue you personally, even if the boys and girls choose not to want him."

"They're children," said Hank. "We're parents, supposed to make responsible decisions."

"Will you decide to let Lesley be a Scoutmaster at Langley Central?" asked Wally.

"That wouldn't be responsible."

"It's the only decision Lesley will accept."

Hank fell silent. He let his gaze drift past Wally and Lesley Xute to the windows and the night outside, where the Cascade Mountains hid. In the other direction was the Saratoga Passage. He would have preferred to be in either place with almost anyone else he knew, than he wanted to be in that room with Lesley Xute.

"Then it's decided," said Wally. "Lesley will attend the next meeting of Langley Central: Hank, you're to give him every welcome. At the end of the evening, the boys and girls, without influence by you, will decide whether they want Lesley to be a Scoutmaster. You can tell me the next morning what they decide."

A long self-satisfied smile stretched through the face of Lesley Xute. He stood up from his chair, towering over Hank as he only could when he was standing and Hank remained seated. Lesley might have been the first to stand so he could.

Lesley remained there, prolonging the moment, before slowly stepping from the chair. Every step unnecessarily slow, he moved towards the door.

Opening the door, he paused and turned around, again looking at Hank still seated at the table. Lesley smiled, not with the kindness of other people's smiles but with a private boastfulness, reserving all his kindness for himself. "I will see you this Wednesday," he told Hank.

Hank simply stared at him. He had nothing more to say to him or not say. Lesley walked on through the door and away.

Wally remained with Hank at the table. They remained silent, while Hank listened for the silence beyond the open door.

Lesley had surely long gone, when Wally spoke again. "I know how you feel, Hank," said Wally. "I feel the same, but we haven't any choice. I touched base today with a buddy in Portland, who said a Korean family and a Pakistani family withdrew their sons from Scouts when Lesley Xute became their leader, but the other leaders had to accept him. We can't let moral matters affect our judgment."

"What else should affect our judgment, Wally?"

"We have to follow the rules, the new rules," insisted Wally. "Keep your morality at home, where I keep mine. There's no person like Lesley Xute in my family, as I know there's none in yours."

"If the Boy Scouts aren't moral, then who is?"

"Scouts, Hank," Wally corrected him. "We stopped being Boy Scouts in 2018."

"They're still boys and the girls are still girls, Wally. They won't feel safe without leaders trying to live moral lives, expecting morality in each other. We ought to provide them more than games to play and camping trips. We ought to provide them moral leadership."

"Leave that to their parents, Hank, like those Korean and Pakistani parents. We're here to provide them games to play and camping trips."

"I want my sons' Scout leaders to reinforce the moral leadership my wife and I provide at home," Hank persisted. "I don't want them undermining it with immorality."

Wally started to stand. "You're a dying breed, Hank," he said. "I wish you weren't, but you are." Wally started to depart, before turning back to Hank. "Lesley told me you had a moose head on the wall of your living room."

The moose head was a strange point of conversation, away from Hank's home. It had been an even stranger point for Lesley to have made in conversation with Wally.

"I'd love to find one of those for my living room," remarked Wally, before departing. Hank remained alone.

Slowly, Hank rose, switched off the lights in the room, and closed the door. Ordinarily, he'd have said "Good night" to either of the owners of the Saratoga Inn, but he wasn't in the mood for pleasantries.

Instead, he ambled home. There, he told Abi the outcome of the meeting.

"We can't have a person like Lesley Xute leading the Scouts," she told him. "We can't have him spending time around our sons, or our friends' sons, or our friends' daughters. We can't pretend he's a role model to our children."

"He might have some attributes," said Hank. "Everybody does."

"Not everybody," said Abi, "but even if he does, we can't pick and choose the messages he'll convey to the children."

"What can we do?" asked Hank. "These decisions aren't made by people knowing best. They're made by people knowing least."

"We can withdraw our boys if he's a leader," answered Abi. "I know other parents who'll withdraw their sons, and their daughters. The children won't want him."

"Ours won't," said Hank, "but other children aren't taught what we know. They're likely to accept him without a thought, simply because he wants to be a leader."

"I'll see who I can talk to."

"I as good as said we wouldn't influence the children."

"Why ever not?" asked Abi. "Everybody else influences them."

"I as good as gave Wally Bowden my word."

Abi shook her head. "Your word," she said. "You keep your quaint old-world morality when nobody else does. Lesley Xute doesn't."

Hank nodded. "That's no reason for me not to keep it."

After a moment's hesitation, she put her hand on his arm. "You're not really the only person left with morality," she told him, before smiling. "I'm stuck with it, too."

Wednesday evening, as they always did, Hank and his two sons arrived early at the church to open up the Multi-Purpose Room. The uniforms, scarves, and caps they wore meant a little less to Hank that evening, although neither he nor Abi had told their sons very much about the man who'd visit them that night. All Hank told them was that he wanted to become one of their Scoutmasters and that the boys and girls would decide whether he would. That was all he'd told the other leaders.

"We've never before voted whether to accept a new Scout leader," Hank's oldest son pointed out.

"We've never before had a person wanting to be a Scoutmaster who was not already a parent," Hank answered, "or whose children joined when he joined because they'd all moved home to Langley."

Other boys and girls in their uniforms, scarves, and caps arrived. Other leaders with their children came.

Punctually at seven o'clock, Lesley arrived wearing a Scoutmaster's uniform, with the badges of a troop in Portland, scarf, and cap. They seemed so clean and colorful as to be new; Hank expected Lesley to have owned several of each, which he wore only while they remained pristine, before buying the next. Lesley carried two large boxes barely able to remain in his arms, before he set them on a table.

The boys and girls clamored around him. "I'm Lesley," he told them, removing from a large box a small box and then another small box he proffered to one child and then another. "I've brought you all some gifts." Children accepting their gifts from Lesley stepped away, allowing another child and then another to take their gifts.

Opening the boxes, children received new telephones,

electronic drones, and other gifts. Hank watched uncomfortably, as the children, his sons among them, eagerly examined their expensive new possessions. If Hank could have stopped what was happening before him then he would have, but he didn't think he could, not without alienating himself from every child who'd not received a gift and inviting another meeting with Wally Bowden.

The other leaders around the room also stood watching Lesley distributing those gifts. They stood dressed in their uniforms somewhat worn in comparison to Lesley Xute's uniform, in their various stages of getting ready for the evening.

Lesley finished handing boxes to every child. He then offered a box to Hank.

"No, thank you," answered Hank. If the other leaders minded not being offered gifts, they didn't show it.

"Boys and girls," Lesley called to them. "Would you like me to help your current leaders lead you? We could go to Alaska or Idaho. We could see the Rocky Mountains!"

"Yes!" called out one boy.

"Yes!" said Hank's youngest son.

The children gathered around Lesley, who put his arms around the boys' shoulders closest to him. His head leant a little towards them, almost touching them. "I have more gifts," he said.

"No," Hank interrupted, stepping towards them. "Boys and girls, you shouldn't accept gifts from strangers. Keep what you have if you want to, but no more."

"Why?" a girl asked. "That isn't fair."

"Men shouldn't offer gifts to children," Hank explained, "when those children aren't theirs or their relatives."

"Why?" the girl asked again. "Lesley isn't a stranger. He's our new leader."

Hank thought long about the words to use, to the dozens of young eyes watching him. They mattered more than Lesley's eyes, brashly studying him. "This man has no children," Hank told them. "He doesn't have a wife, and I don't think he ever will. I don't think he'll ever have children of his own."

"That's sad," said another girl.

"It is sad," said Hank, "but I'd be certain he could find a wife if he wanted to find one. He could have children of his own, but he doesn't want them."

The children stood silently. One moved a little away from the huddle around Lesley, and then another. Hank's elder son broke from the pack altogether and moved towards his father.

His younger brother soon followed. Other boys and girls soon also followed, until they all stood scattered around Hank. They weren't close to him, aside from his sons, but they stood much closer to Hank than they stood to Lesley. In their hands were still the presents they'd received from Lesley.

"What about my gifts?" Lesley asked the boys and girls. "Don't you like my gifts?"

Again they all stood silently, before Hank's elder son moved towards the table on which Lesley had placed his two big boxes. Hank's son popped his gift back into its small box and rested the box back in one of the big boxes.

Hank's younger son was among the boys and girls soon doing the same, returning their gifts to the small boxes in which they'd come and the small boxes to Lesley's big boxes. When all the gifts were back in the big boxes, the boys and girls again stood scattered around Hank.

"Don't you want to see Alaska and Idaho?" Lesley asked the boys and girls. "There are so many places I can show you."

Hank's eldest son answered him. "We can see those places and other places with the leaders we've got."

Lesley looked around at each boy and girl. He looked at Hank and every other leader. The children and leaders all stood motionless, watching him.

Slowly, Lesley turned and walked back to the table and boxes. He looked over them for a moment, before looking back at Hank. "I could tell Wally Bowden that you turned the children against me."

"Have I said anything untrue?" asked Hank.

"I could insist upon meeting all the parents," persisted Lesley.

"They would have already heard from their children what happened tonight."

"I could still sue," continued Lesley.

"Do you still want to be a leader here," asked Hank, "to boys and girls who said your gifts aren't going to be enough?"

Lesley continued to stare at Hank. If he was thinking of more things to say, or threats to make, then Hank was ready. The boys, girls, and leaders continued watching Lesley, quieter than the boys and girls normally were.

Sluggishly, Lesley turned around to the table and the two big cardboard boxes. The boxes weren't packed as neatly and efficiently as they'd been when Lesley brought them there, but he collected them back into his arms.

Barely holding those boxes in place against his chest, and his Scoutmaster uniform, Lesley again turned to Hank. "Do you care what happens to me?" he asked.

"I care," said Hank. "What does your father think of your lifestyle?"

Lesley turned his face away. "I don't know my father," he answered. "He left my mother soon after I was born, as she reminds me every time I speak with her."

Quietly, incrementally, Lesley carried his two big boxes towards the doorway. Hank imagined Lesley offering the boys and girls a tiding before he left, but he didn't. "I'm sorry about your father, Lesley," said Hank.

Lesley continued towards the doorway. Langley Central Scouts might or might not see Alaska and Idaho, but Hank expected never to see Lesley Xute again.

With Lesley about to pass through that doorway, Hank called to him. "Lesley," he said.

Lesley stopped. He didn't turn around.

"If you want my advice," said Hank, "forget the Scouts, for now, forget the gifts. I hope you find some peace of mind and get yourself a girlfriend, then a wife, then a family. When you're the type of person children want to be around without the need for gifts, instead of someone people suffer because you force yourself upon them, then you might feel glad for what happened here tonight. We can then talk about you and your children joining us in Langley Central."

Still facing the door, Lesley laughed. It was an exaggerated laugh of unconvincing bellicosity, which might have been more unsettling if that was all Hank knew of him. Before leaving and still facing the doorway, Lesley spoke a final time, just loud enough for Hank to hear him. "I don't want your advice."

4 GIRL SCOUTS

Morality becoming obsolete didn't stop people telling Americans what to do. It just meant the things they told Americans to do weren't premised upon those Americans' best interests or any shared interests, but upon their self interests, as they saw them.

A century earlier, soon after Lord Baden Powell founded the Boy Scouts in Britain, he and his sister founded the Girl Guides. After meeting Lord Baden Powell, Juliette Gordon Low founded the American Girl Guides in Georgia in 1912. Eventually spreading nationwide, the American Girl Guides were soon renamed Girl Scouts to reflect America's pioneering history, as Girl Guides weren't named in other countries.

Unlike the Scouts, formerly known as Boy Scouts, two decades into the twenty-first century, the Girl Scouts hadn't admitted boys. No men or women clamored for their sons to join the Girl Scouts as women had clamored for other women's daughters to join the Boy Scouts.

Like the Scouts, the Girl Scouts engaged in community activities. Girl Scouts were probably best known for selling cookies, which was a community activity, quite apart from raising funds.

Away from public eyes, but not from birds and animals, were the camps. By day, the girls could hike, canoe, or fish, much as boys and girls could in Scouts. Perhaps more so than the Scouts, Girl Scouts engaged in crafts and other calm activities around their campground cabins and tents.

By night, after eating their dinners of variable delectability and before sleeping in their tents or, more comfortably, cabins, Girl Scouts sat around campfires. Keeping warm or just being together, campfires were times for toasting marshmallows and telling ghost stories through the flames and embers around which they sat. Girl Scouts sang the Girl Scout songs they sang every camp and other songs they also seemed to sing at every camp.

As states did throughout America, West Virginia offered several State Parks in which people camped. Twelve girls from Girl Scout

Troop 3984 in Martinsburg, along with three of their leaders, undertook a five-night camp amidst the valleys and mountains towards Harpers Ferry. An ordinary girl, she liked to think, with long blonde hair she kept free from knots, but tied into a ponytail on camps, Avril Pemberton had been a member of the troop, a Cadette, for more than two years. Soon, she would turn fourteen years of age and progress to Seniors.

Two of the three leaders were mothers to girls on the camp. Only Sadie was not a mother to any of the girls, or anyone else.

The girls were supposed to know only the leaders' first names, but the girls all knew Sadie's family name was Bluett. (With so many mothers retaining their maiden names, knowing the daughters' family names didn't tell other girls the mothers' family names, unless other girls asked. They did.)

Sadie might have been thirty years of age, with an athletic gait and dark brown hair. The mothers wore little make-up, much less than the girls wore, but Sadie wore least of all. She might have worn none at all, at least among the girls, unless she applied the make-up that made her seem like she didn't apply any. (Avril's mother often told her that the best make-up was make-up that no one noticed, but Avril did not believe her, not at Avril's age.)

The girls had decided between themselves that Sadie didn't have a boyfriend, a little embarrassed to have been so candid, if only among themselves. She wasn't ugly, but she really wasn't very pretty, they thought, aside other women of her age. Her jaw was a little square and her nose a little crooked, but none of that was any reason to dislike her. They might have been more reasons to like her.

For being younger than the other leaders and for being equally unrelated to all the girls, as well as being perpetually cheerful and friendly, Sadie was the most popular of the leaders of their troop, although none of the leaders were unpopular. Only some of the older women the girls encountered from other troops or from the Girl Scout Council, who rarely seemed to smile and too often chastised them, could be unpopular.

Each night of their five-night camp, the girls and leaders sat around a campfire in comfortable jackets and jeans, keeping warm; uniforms were for events among other people and meetings back home in Martinsburg. They sang, and in their most patriotic moments broke into a rare song, other than the Girl Scout songs, to which they all knew all the words: *Take Me Home, Country Roads*.

At camps, meetings, and every other time Avril saw her, Sadie carried a smartphone, as most people did, but Sadie spent more time with hers than other people spent with theirs. Every so often, and sometimes quite frequently, Sadie studied the shining screen; at night, it lit Sadie's face better than any campfire did. She'd read, and sometimes type secret messages (secret from the girls) into it to send away, far from the girls.

Once in a while, Sadie slipped away to a quiet place, or what had been a quiet place, from which Avril could only hear her indecipherable murmuring of one side of a conversation. It might be brief, lasting only a minute or two, or continue for as much as an hour, before Sadie returned to the troop. "Work," she might explain, although most of the time she didn't say anything, before again joining whatever activity was underway.

When conversation slowed around the campfire, and it rarely did, the leaders ignited it again. The fourth night of the camp that week, after a small lull in the conversations, Sadie asked a question of the girls: "What does everyone want to do when she grows up?"

In answer to Sadie's question, one girl around the campfire raised her hand. Jolene always raised her hand before speaking to leaders.

"Yes, Jolene," said Sadie.

"I want to be a doctor," said Jolene, "like my father."

Girls nodded. So did Sadie. "Doctors are very important," said Sadie. "You can help a lot of people. You can go to Africa and help the mothers with their babies."

"What does your mother do?" Avril asked Jolene.

"She doesn't do anything."

Girls laughed. Sadie smiled.

"Doesn't she raise you?" asked Avril.

"That isn't anything."

Avril looked towards the two other leaders around the campfire, both mothers to girls there, sitting together. Avril thought might have had something to say in response to Jolene, but they did not react. Instead, they continued quietly watching all the girls, as they normally did. Avril didn't know whether they were employed outside their family homes or not. It was not her place to ask.

"You can do anything you want to do," Sadie told the girls,

looking around the group, "anything."

"Unless it's illegal," said another girl, Leah.

A couple of girls giggled. "Now," Sadie told them all, "some girls, some women, have done some very impressive things that were illegal."

"What things?" asked Leah.

Sadie nodded. "When the time comes for each of you to decide what you want to do," she smiled, "you decide, and then think about the laws. Some women broke the law so you could all vote one day."

"Who did?" asked Leah. "Wasn't that a long time ago?"

"Aren't Girl Scouts supposed to keep the law?" asked Jolene. "Aren't we supposed to keep not just the Scouts' Law but other laws, too?"

"All I'm saying," said Sadie, "is don't automatically let laws you didn't make stop you from doing something, if that's what you want, and if you know that what you're doing is right." She then smiled, with a big, long smile that couldn't help but make others smile. "I did."

"What did you do?" asked Leah.

Sadie looked at her. The girls sat perfectly hushed listening for her answer. "I'll tell you when you're older," she smiled.

Avril wondered what mischievous or other deeds Sadie had done. She also wondered whether Sadie would ever tell them.

"Now, Leah," Sadie asked her. "You sound like you want to be a lawyer when you leave school."

"I do," smiled Leah. All the girls and leaders laughed.

"There are many important groups always looking for lawyers to help them," Sadie told her. "I think the United Nations would like your help, but so would contraception rights and immigrant advocacy groups. I would help them if I could."

Leah nodded, before slowly venturing her next remark. "I thought I would like to work for a big company," she said, "with travel and expense accounts."

Sadie smiled; she always smiled. "You can do that, Leah," Sadie told her. "If you study hard and work hard, you can do anything you set your heart on doing."

Another girl raised her hand. "I want to be an astronaut," said Violet. "I want to be the first person to set foot on the planet Mars."

Some girls sniggered. Others laughed.

"Don't snicker," Sadie told them. "This is what I mean. Why shouldn't any of you be the first person to walk on Mars: taking one small step as a woman but a giant leap for womankind?"

"Shouldn't that be personkind?" asked Violet.

Sadie looked at her for a moment, before nodding. "Yes, Violet," she said, "personkind."

Other girls spoke of their career ambitions, to varying degrees of interest from each other, before it became Avril's turn to speak. "I don't want a career," she said.

Some girls laughed. Sadie laughed louder than all of them.

"I want to marry a man like my father and raise a family," said Avril.

It seemed every girl was laughing, as was Sadie. The two other leaders, the two mothers, sat quietly.

"You must be the first girl to talk like that for fifty years," laughed Sadie.

"I'm not," insisted Avril.

Sadie became a little serious, with only the barest hint of her smile remaining. "Who told you to say that all you want is to be a mother?" she inquired of Avril. "Do you say that at school? Do you say that in other places?"

"No," said Avril. "People keep talking about careers as we grow up, but you're the first person to ask me what I want to do."

Sadie looked around the group, her smile returning. "I'm glad we've aired your dirty linen, then," she said, turning back to Avril. "Now, we can all clean it for you. Wouldn't you like a career? What does your father do?"

"What he calls another pointless job in another pointless company," answered Avril.

"He should change job," Sadie told her. "He should change company."

"He has," answered Avril, "from one pointless job in a pointless company to another, and then another."

"My job is very exciting," said Sadie. "I can take you there next week to show you."

Avril wasn't interested in such an excursion, any more than she'd been interested in visiting her father's place of work. She was much too polite to say so.

"Don't you want to work?" asked Sadie. "Are you lazy?"

"Being a wife and mother isn't lazy," answered Avril. "My father says there are lots of lazy people in companies, but they hide it and pretend to work. Nobody's paying close enough attention to them to see it, probably for fear of being caught being just as lazy."

"Aren't you very intelligent, then?" persisted Sadie. "You've got to be intelligent to work in a company."

Avril shook her head. "My father says there are many unintelligent people in companies, but their jobs are all so pointless, nobody notices."

"You need a different father, Avril Pemberton," said Sadie. "Your father is a very bad influence upon you. What does your mother say? What does she do?"

"She doesn't want two people in the house with pointless jobs," answered Avril. "I don't know whether she'd call hers a job, looking after us all, but it isn't pointless."

"It is pointless," snapped Sadie, as Avril had never before seen her. Other girls jerked back around the campfire, as Sadie looked around at each of them. "You should know it's pointless," she told them. "You must know that." Sadie looked again at Avril. "Your mother doesn't get paid," Sadie told her, "making her life slavery."

"Whatever my father gets paid," insisted Avril, quoting her mother without needing to say so, "my mother gets paid. He says that the only purpose of his job is to bring money home to my mother, but that's more of a purpose than the jobs of men and women without families to feed."

Sadie again looked around at the girls, sitting in their campfire circle. "I don't know what's wrong with Avril's mother," Sadie told them, shaking her head. "Somebody should speak with her."

Nobody said anything more after that, not loud enough for Avril to hear anyway. The girls stared into the fading flames and dying embers, occasionally whispering between themselves. Nobody whispered with Anvil. The three leaders watched the girls, with Sadie watching Avril every time that Avril noticed her.

Early the next morning, the last full day of the camp, the girls and leaders readied themselves for the day, much as they'd done every day on camp. When Avril was alone, brushing her hair, Jolene approached her. "You were very brave to say what you said last night," Jolene told her. "I could never do that, not even here, so far from people."

Avril stopped brushing her hair. "I know we're not supposed to admit it," she asked Jolene, "but is marrying and having children what you really want to do when you grow up?"

Jolene continued looking at Avril, before looking around them. Avril didn't think anyone else was near them, but perhaps someone was. "I don't want people laughing at me," said Jolene, "the way they laughed at you."

"What would girls say if nobody was going to laugh at them?" asked Avril. "What would they say without people telling them what to say?"

Sadie approached them. Jolene slipped away.

Only Sadie stood with Avril. "Women gave their lives so you don't have to be a housewife," Sadie told Avril.

"I never asked anyone to give her life for me not to be a wife and mother," insisted Avril. "I thought we're supposed to have choices to do whatever we want to do: to sit in a dingy factory or office if we want to sit in a dingy factory or office, or to live life in a family home we make if that is what we want?"

"What's the use in having choices if you don't take them?" asked Sadie.

"What's the use in having choices we don't want?"

"Choices change," said Sadie. "All the other girls want them."

Avril looked around at those girls, standing around the campground, getting ready for the day. She didn't know if they were sincere in what they'd said, or if they'd ever considered words like hers the night just passed.

A familiar buzz sounded from Sadie's clothes, whereby she whipped her smartphone from her pocket. With one hand holding the device and the index finger of her other hand tapping the screen, she studied the screen.

Avril was close enough to see there were words on the screen, without being close enough to read them. The words could have been right side up from her perspective, but she still couldn't have read them.

Sadie's index finger danced over the screen. When it finished, her eyes remained there, presumably checking, before she slipped her smartphone back into her pocket.

After eating breakfast, the twelve girls and their three leaders packed food and bottles of water into their small daypacks. Those daypacks on either or both of their shoulders, they hiked along the river's edge. They walked in a column one girl wide, except sometimes where the trail was wide enough for two girls to walk beside each other. One leader walked at the front, another at the back, and the third could be anywhere front, back, or in between.

Sometimes the girls talked between themselves. Most of the time, they saved their energy for walking and their concentration upon the river and the mountains. A little more often, the leaders talked between themselves, normally about where they were headed or when they might get there, in so far as Avril heard.

Interrupting Avril's concentration, Sadie's voice called from the back of the pack behind her: "Move along, Avril Pemberton."

Avril had thought that she was walking no slower, or quicker, than other girls walked, but she sped up anyway. She passed another girl.

A few minutes later, Sadie called out, again. "Come on, Avril Pemberton," she said. "You're slowing everybody up."

Avril reached the front of the group, with the leader walking there. The leader smiled, without speaking.

Again, from far behind her, Sadie called out. "Avril Pemberton," she said. Avril wondered how Sadie even knew where she was from so far back, if indeed Sadie knew where Avril was. Sadie couldn't know how fast she walked. "We'll all miss lunch if you can't keep up!"

Avril looked at the leader beside whom she walked. They both walked a little quicker.

The troop stopped for lunch at a small clearing by a cliff ledge, overlooking the river. The girls and two of the leaders sat down, opened their packs, and removed their packet lunches and water bottles. Sadie stood at the top of the cliff, looking away from the troop. Facing the river and mountains across the river, Sadie reached out her arms like a bird ready to fly. "I want to take flight," she cried out to the wilderness.

Sadie did things like that. Starting to eat and drink, the girls and other leaders watched her. Avril couldn't see whether Sadie's eyes were open or closed.

Facing the wilderness, Sadie stood atop that cliff for several more moments, before turning around. She faced the girls and other two leaders watching her, and dropped her arms. "You'll understand when you're older," she told the girls.

Avril wondered whether the mother leaders, being older than the girls, understood. They didn't indicate one way or the other.

After checking her smartphone, Sadie returned to her daypack, from which she removed her lunch and water bottles. There, alone, Avril left the other girls and approached her. "Why are you picking on me?" asked Avril, speaking softly enough that only Sadie heard her.

Sadie replied in her usual sound of voice. "You were too slow moving today."

"I was faster than anyone else," Avril protested.

"Girl Scouts don't lie, Avril Pemberton," Sadie told her. "I wonder if the Seniors will let you join them when you leave Cadettes, knowing that you lie. They don't have to let you join them. Then you won't be in Girl Scouts anymore. I might have to have a word with them."

Sadie started to eat. Avril looked at her, unable to guess what to say. Saying anything probably wouldn't help.

Slowly, Avril turned away. She walked slowly back to the other girls.

After lunch, with all their materials and rubbish in their daypacks, leaving nothing behind, the girls and leaders resumed their hike along the trail. Again, Avril walked with a leader, not Sadie, at the front of the pack. Ahead of them, lying curled and motionless on the ground in the middle of the trail, Avril saw something. "What's that?" she whispered, as she stopped walking.

The leader with her also stopped. The girls behind them stopped. The leader's voice was also hushed. "It's a snake," answered the leader, also whispering.

"Ah," gasped the girl immediately behind them, drawing Avril's attention to her. Leah covered her mouth, as if that could bring back the sound she'd made, before turning around to the stationary girl behind her. "There's a snake up ahead," Leah whispered.

"Ah," exclaimed the next girl, before she too turned around. The quiet message became its own procession rippling through the troop, while the girls hearing the news inched forward for a chance to see. Some of them standing on their toes to see past other girls, they slowly set their eyes upon the snake.

Avril turned back towards the snake, unmoved since last she'd seen it. The snake was less than a yard long, curled into a clumsy circle less than a foot wide. Pictures that Avril and the other girls had seen of snakes at their meetings in Martinsburg, so far away from there, came back to mind. The snake was thick and black, which might have meant it wasn't dangerous. Now that those pictures mattered so much to her, Avril could not recall anything important about them. In all their camps and other times outdoors, Avril had never before encountered a snake.

Most importantly, if the snake moved towards her, Avril's instinct was to flee, crashing into the girls behind her who'd also flee, crashing into each other. That wasn't what the girls had been taught to do, back in Martinsburg. Avril remembered that.

"Don't move," whispered the mother leader beside Avril. "Even if it comes towards us, stand still. Let it pass."

Avril knew the advice was sound. She didn't know whether, if the snake should come towards them, she or any other girls would follow that advice.

To the sides of them, more girls slowly appeared, inching no closer to the snake than any other girl. Soon, Sadie came bustling through the troop, until she stopped by Avril.

Sadie's voice too was softer than she normally spoke. "Think of that snake being like marriage and motherhood," she whispered to Avril. "The snake appears harmless, like something you can touch and play with, but it might bite and kill you. Do you want to handle that?"

All the conversations had become whispers, in sight of the snake. Avril continued watching the snake, while answering Sadie. "Would you say the same thing to boys about marriage and fatherhood?" asked Avril.

"I keep away from boys," said Sadie. "Boys become men."

"Don't you have a boyfriend," Avril asked Sadie, "a husband?"

"What I have," insisted Sadie, whispering as loudly as any person could while still whispering, "won't ever get in the way of my career."

The other girls and leaders stood silently. "Isn't your career the snake?" asked Avril. "Mightn't it bite and kill you?"

Those closest to Sadie and Avril could surely hear Sadie as well as Avril could. "You can move the snake, Avril," whispered Sadie. "It isn't very big."

"It's big enough."

"Don't you want to prove you're smart?" asked Sadie. "Don't you want to prove you can work?"

"Leaders should deal with snakes."

"I've got a career," insisted Sadie. "I can't afford to get bitten; I might have to take time from work. The other girls will have their careers. They can't afford to get hurt."

"You're horrible," said Avril.

"I'm trying to teach you a lesson," insisted Sadie, "for your own good. Nobody else has taught you the lesson so I must, or have you just not learnt it from other people?"

"I'm not going near a snake," maintained Avril, no less forcibly than Sadie had been.

Sadie turned to face the girls in their cluster. "Avril Pemberton is too scared to move the snake," Sadie told them.

Avril interjected. "Isn't everyone scared?" she asked them.

Sadie answered. "Other girls are more important," she told Avril.

One girl gasped, facing the snake. Avril and the other girls and leaders turned to see the snake's head slowly moving, its body following, stretched out from its curls over the uneven ground. It slithered into the forest.

The girls and leaders stepped back from the side of the trail to which the snake had gone, without yet stepping forward again. For several minutes, they studied the forest by the trail, especially the forest nearest them. Not just the snake they had already seen but another snake could appear at any time.

Eventually, resuming their hike along the trail appeared no more dangerous than standing still. "You go ahead, Avril," Sadie told her.

Instead, without saying a word, a mother leader stepped ahead of them and walked along the trail ahead of them. Avril walked close behind her, no longer looking at the scenery but studying every spot of ground and tree for snakes. The other girls and leaders followed.

That mother leader was Violet's mother, Irma. When the trail was wide enough, Avril walked beside her, initiating their conversation. "How did you feel to hear Sadie talk like that last night about women and careers?" Avril asked her. "How did you feel to hear Jolene say her mother didn't do anything?"

"When Violet was very young," answered Irma, as they walked, "she answered a school project about careers for people by talking about me, at home, caring for Violet and her brothers. She wrote some beautiful text, collected some lovely photographs, and brought everything together into a poster I thought was very good, but her teacher failed her. Raising families wasn't what Irma and the other students were supposed to write about."

"That wasn't fair," said Avril.

Irma pushed a small branch out of her way, holding it so that it wouldn't flick back and hit the girl behind her. That girl took the branch and held it for the girl behind her.

Avril resumed her conversation with Irma, walking again. "Did any of the boys in Violet's class talk about caring for their children?"

"Boys know that marriage and fatherhood don't save them from getting jobs," explained Irma. "Even the boys whose fathers spend most of their days raising them and their sisters because their mothers can earn more money, some of those fathers can't get jobs at all, or because their mothers aren't around, know how peculiar their circumstances are."

Avril laughed. "My brothers know," she said, "my father knows."

"Violet learnt from that experience and others like it," continued Irma. "She does want a career now, although the career she wants changes every day, sometimes several times a day, depending on who she's talking to. I also learnt from those experiences, so I keep mum."

Late in the afternoon, back at the campsite and before dinner was to be prepared, the three leaders held another of the meetings among themselves they often held. That left the girls to do as they pleased, as they were often left. This afternoon, the girls gathered together.

Leah was the first to speak with Avril. "You've really upset Sadie," said Leah. "I want us all to be cheerful again."

Jolene was the next to address Avril. "Why can't you tell Sadie what she wants to hear?" she asked. "Tell her you've decided upon a career. It doesn't matter what career. Tell her you want to be president of the United States. Tell her anything. She's nicer than she's been to you since you made so much last night of getting married and having a family."

"She asked me and I answered," countered Avril.

"Sadie mightn't mind you marrying and having a family," said Violet, "if you convince her that they're less important than a career."

That night, the last night of a camp, was normally a night for festivity, celebrating all that the girls had done throughout their time away. This night, everything felt a little sullen. While other girls collected wood for the campfire, Avril approached Sadie. "Why are you so hostile to families?" Avril asked her.

"You should be, too."

"Why?"

"All I have is my career, and I'm content," insisted Sadie. "I want you to be content."

"Are you content?" asked Avril. "I'm not so certain anymore."

"Can't you let it go, Avril? Can't you trust me and the other girls that you should pursue your career?"

"If you give me reasons, then I'll listen," persisted Avril.

"What reasons have you given me for wanting marriage and motherhood?" Sadie retorted.

"I'm not trying to persuade you to my point of view," said Avril, "but you're picking on me for mine."

Sadie shook her head. "You've got to toughen up if you want to survive," she said. "I hate to say it, but you've got to be less like a girl and more like a man."

"Is that what your career is like?" asked Avril. "Is that your life, now?"

Sadie's tone of voice softened. "We should be talking about you."

Her gentler tone was harder to challenge than her belligerence had been. "What does your mother say?" Avril asked her.

Sadie looked up into the sky, so far and wide as sky could be from West Virginian mountains, far from the lights of other people. "Whatever my mother says about anything," said Sadie, "she doesn't say to me."

"What does your father say?"

"Ha," scoffed Sadie. "He, I know, doesn't say anything to anyone, especially not me."

"I'm sorry," said Avril, "even if I don't know what I'm feeling sorry for."

Sadie continued looking around the sky. "I was young," she said, "as young as you are now." The light from the sky reflected in a tear in her eye. "I believed adults telling me what I'm telling you."

Avril stood silently. It was not her time to speak.

"Don't you see?" asked Sadie, looking back at her. "My career is all I have. If you're right and I am wrong, then I have nothing. Is that what you want?"

"What is your career?" asked Avril. "What do you do, that you want me to see you do next week?"

"Nothing," said Sadie, shaking her head. "I don't do anything, but I'm very well paid for doing it. I do it every day that I'm not helping with Girl Scouts, and I do it very well, everybody says."

Sadie looked back to the sky. Avril waited for Sadie to speak again, but she didn't. She waited for her to look at her again, but she didn't.

That familiar buzz sounded from Sadie's clothes. From a pocket, she removed her smartphone and turned away. In the cooling night, Avril left her alone.

Gloomily, perhaps, but certainly privately and withdrawn, Sadie performed only the tasks required of her as a leader through that evening and then the last day of the camp, finally heading home to Martinsburg that afternoon. She and Avril had no more conversations.

Avril told her parents about the camp and most of the things that Sadie had said and done. She mentioned the snake along the trail, although hearing herself describe Sadie's actions then, they didn't sound too bad. Ultimately, the leaders and girls had left the snake alone, as Avril's father said they were right to do.

Apparently, it was one of the mother leaders who reported Sadie's actions with the snake and Avril to the Girl Scout Council. Whether that was Irma, Violet's mother, Avril never learnt. The Council reported to Avril and Avril's parents that Sadie insisted that she knew the snake was harmless when she suggested that Avril move it. She said she only wanted to challenge Avril and the other girls. She wanted them to be brave.

Avril wasn't in a position to talk about the thoughts in Sadie's head. She confirmed the truth of what had happened on the trail, reported by the mother leader.

The Girl Scouts promptly expelled Sadie from their ranks of leaders. She still had her career, and her smartphone.

5 THE BELLE

As children grew, through the time of old America, the differences between boys and girls captivated them. Nothing mattered more to young men and women than attracting each other, specifically those particular men and women they each found the most attractive. They dressed and groomed themselves accordingly, even when not admitting it, while every hint of encouragement from the objects of their desires excited them. Through every personal task and national objective, including the direst of national threats and calamities, courtship remained paramount in their thinking. Why survive a threat or calamity if not for love and marriage?

Two decades into twenty-first century America, men and women pursued something less than sustaining love, although they might call their newfound desires love. At their worst, the objects of their desires were their individual selves, not in deep perpetuity amidst their families, communities, and nation but for the superficial moment. Their newly paramount desires often weren't love at all.

Not like that, her father Landon felt certain, was Trixie Evans, although he never quite knew what she thought as she sat in the swinging seat on their front porch. Their family home was in Garyville, Louisiana, along the north bank of another bend in the Mississippi River, which a levee for the most part hid from sight. Trixie was sixteen years of age and very pretty, her parents often told her.

Their home, like many in Garyville, was modern, but the best known house in Garyville was the nineteenth-century San Francisco Plantation. It had ceased being a family home in 1974, when the widowed Mrs. Thompson vacated it, before passing through various owners. Following a restoration, the colorful blue-shuttered house and rest of the plantation became a museum. Hosting a debutante ball in the Sugar Mill Pavilion, which already hosted weddings, seemed a very good idea, thought Landon, feeling a little proud for having thought if it. His family and friends agreed.

From that time of old America, debutante balls were still held every year in New Orleans, forty miles away. If Landon could organize his ball, then it would be the first in Garyville, so far as anyone could remember.

Debutante balls weren't unique to the American South or even to America, but they connoted the old American South, at least to older Louisianans. They'd initially been for the children of the rich and aristocratic, before becoming available to the children of all. They heralded young women coming out, debuting into adult society when society was adult. Flaunting their female beauty in fine gowns and dresses, they declared to the world that they were old and mature enough to marry. No longer were they the little girls who could only dream of wedding days, who would never dress like that, not properly.

Most of all, those debutantes declared their capacity to marry to the young bachelors (often debutants themselves) old and mature enough to marry them. Traditionally, the debutantes invited particular young bachelors to the ball. No less than were the young women attracting young men, young men were attracting young women.

Men wanted femininity in their women: beauty and grace. Women wanted masculinity in their men: strength and charm, alluding to their capacity to provide. They both wanted reliability and manners in the other. All of that would underpin the families they'd make, for which they each needed the other. Those families underpinned communities.

If marriage was a man or woman's greatest success, then their children were their greatest achievements. They were the reasons behind everything they were and did: not just their love and marriage but every home and accumulation of goods and wealth, every accomplishment from their personal through their familial to their national. Parents preparing their children for life included, above all else, preparing them for marriage and parenthood, with all that those great markers of life entailed. Watching their bachelor sons and debut daughters at the ball, so well dressed and behaved, those parents declared their tasks, thus far at any rate, complete.

Old fashioned that all might have been, but Landon and his wife still thought that way. Sixteen years of age wasn't really old enough to marry, not two decades into twenty-first century

America, but it was old enough for Trixie to join adult society, as it was in Garyville. The debutante ball her father planned would be her excuse, she told him, to invite Roscoe Jansen. A young man a year older than she was and who also lived in Garyville, Roscoe worked at the oil refinery. Landon hadn't met him.

Trixie's brother Caleb was eighteen years of age. Finding a skill that must once have abounded in Louisiana but had become rare, at least in Garyville, he felt, Caleb would need to coax Amity Whest to invite him to the ball.

Their father Landon was not the most obvious person to convene a debutante ball, or any other celebration of personal beauty. At the left side of his face was a crimson birthmark, to which even the most polite of people could not help but glance when first they met him, even if they politely never mentioned it. At various times, he'd tried to cover it with a beard, but beards never grew easily on him. The scattered scraggly hairs growing from his face only made his birthmark more unsightly. If anything had eased the birthmark's impact on his face through his aging life, it was the Louisiana sun.

What remained for all to see was Landon, and he was never proud of his appearance, but he was proud of his two children. For them, and especially his daughter, along with all the other young people in and around Garyville, he would convene a ball.

Monday afternoon, in the otherwise unoccupied Sugar Mill Pavilion, Landon presented his plan. Sitting at white chairs around one of the many identical round dining tables were seven local merchants. They could seem an eclectic group of men and women, but they all operated businesses in and around Garyville and all cared passionately about the town and people.

With them at the table was Suellyn Bonnier from the San Francisco Plantation, along with a representative of the St. John the Baptist Parish School Board, since the ball would involve schoolchildren. Also at the table was a woman Landon had not expected to be there. "I've invited Devorah Chodorow to the meeting," explained the school board representative, "because she knows something about dances."

Devorah's face was conspicuously pallid aside the sun-stained faces around the rest of the table, while the blackness of her blouse made the pale open-collar shirts and dresses other people wore seem brighter than they otherwise had been. She dabbed her moistened forehead with a napkin she returned to the table close to her, still holding it, although that day and month were really rather mild. She was probably from the North, thought Landon; even in the Pavilion, Southern humidity affected visitors from Northern climes more than it affected Louisianans.

Walking around the table, Landon described traditional debutante balls for people unfamiliar with them. Pointing to the empty chairs and tables and to the walls and ceiling, he called upon them to picture decorations much like those for wedding receptions.

"The night of the ball," continued Landon, walking towards the main door and raising his voice, "the microphone should be here." He stopped by the door and turned back to his audience in their chairs, some twisted a little to watch him. "A master of ceremony will announce each debutante by name upon her arrival, with her father. My daughter wants to find the most beautiful ball dress she can, but it'll be the girls' beauty they'll be showing off."

His left elbow reached out and bent for a daughter to hold, Landon stepped forward from the door towards the center of the empty polished floor. He stepped in a slow procession of one, as a patient father would.

"Each father will escort his daughter," he explained, "one father and one daughter at a time, unless so many debutantes come they need to form a close procession. All eyes will be upon each debutante, apart from her father's eyes. He'll be watching everybody watching her."

Landon reached the center of the floor. He stopped walking.

"With his parents watching, also dressed resplendently, each young bachelor that each debutante invited will wait here in turn for her," he told the men and women at their table. "My son has never worn a suit, but he says he will for this. He'll also learn to ballroom dance, for when the young men take those debutantes from their fathers."

Landon walked back towards the table, while nodding his or her approval was every man and woman seated there, except one. The expert upon dances sat silent and still.

"The ball should attract people from all 'round the Bayou State," enthused Landon, sitting back in his chair, "who'd never think of going to the big ball in New Orleans." Any profits from the Garyville ball would go to the San Francisco Plantation.

Amidst the smiles, one merchant expressed the table's mood. "I like it, boy," said the operator of the food mart, a largish, older man. "I'm sure as heck gonna muster all the folk I can muster to support ya."

Before Landon could thank him, Devorah Chodorow spoke up. "There are some things to keep in mind," she said, with the speed that came of speaking without what the Northerners called a Southern drawl, but with a Northern twang Landon guessed was New Yorker. (He expected all the city-strangers from the North to be from New York.) "Some of the debutantes, if we have to call them that, won't have fathers. Any person must be able to escort each debutante into the pavilion."

Landon nodded. "I guess debutante balls allow that," he said, looking around for guidance among people who didn't know. "The girls will have uncles and grandfathers, who could escort them."

"Why must we talk only of girls being debutantes?" asked Devorah.

Landon laughed. "Boys can't be debutantes," he said, looking around again at the other people there.

"Why can't boys be debutantes?" asked Devorah.

Landon stared dumbfounded at her: her black, wavy hair and the pallid skin that certain city people, especially from New York, suffered never seeing the sun. She had implicitly denied the premise of debutante balls, so far as Landon understood it. She denied their purpose.

"You shouldn't talk of beauty," continued Devorah.

"If anyone wanted beauty hidden to protect the unbeautiful," said Landon, pointedly touching the birthmark on his face, "it would be me." His words must have taken the men and women around the table aback. "I'm not denying other people their beauty because of my flaws."

"Think of the girls," said Devorah, although Landon wondered whether she thought most about her. "We don't want them feeling excluded because they don't feel beautiful. We don't want girls feeling judged by their looks."

"Are you a mother?" asked Landon. "They judge themselves by their looks. That's how they attract boys."

"Don't you want to mold them into better human beings?" asked Devorah.

Rarely had Landon taken such a quick dislike to a person as

he'd taken to Devorah Chodorow. "They know what makes them better human beings," he told her, "before adults like you corrupt their impressionable minds. Boys dress well when they realize that makes them attractive to girls, who dress to lure the boys, or keep the boys they have. It's all they're interested in at that age and good for them. It's far more sensible than some of the garbage older people fret about." If those last words left their visitor feeling slighted, then Landon would let her feel it.

The mood around the table had once been so receptive to Landon and then supportive of him. It no longer was.

"If we can't find a way to stop debutante balls being beauty contests," said Devorah, "then they'll go the same way as beauty contests: anachronistic in the modern age."

Landon scoffed at her. "If beautiful women or handsome men upset people," he told her, "then those people can be upset. If people are offended by young men and women falling in love then they should be offended. They might learn to make themselves beautiful or handsome, instead of pulling down the women and men who are."

"Boys and girls have different ideas of beauty," insisted Devorah, "according to their orientations."

Landon recognized that word he'd never used, to describe something he'd never had call to mention. "That isn't a problem in Garyville," he said.

"It isn't a problem at all," retorted Devorah.

This was a conversation unlike any that Landon had previously experienced. It was one he had never imagined experiencing in Garyville. "I am sorry," said Landon, "who are you again?"

The School Board representative answered on her behalf. "Devorah is a civil libertarian from New York," he explained.

That explained her, thought Landon. Nothing she said would surprise him anymore.

"I invited Devorah here," continued the School Board representative, "because I've seen schools in other states threatened with problems for convening father-daughter dances; I'm glad she's already mentioned daughters without fathers. I don't want contention happening here, and thought that if we involved civil libertarians from the beginning, we can keep everything harmonious."

Landon looked back at Devorah. "Our little ball in Garyville,

Louisiana brought you all the way from New York?" he asked.

"We'll travel to any corner of any state to defend civil liberties."

"There are debutante balls scattered across America without aggravation."

"You're not aware of the efforts they make to be inclusive of everyone," Devorah explained. "I'm not personally aware, but if anyone complains about any of them to us, then we will investigate. We will take legal action if necessary."

Landon looked around the table at the other men and women. They all sat silently, no longer smiling.

"You shouldn't call the ball traditional," continued Devorah, as much to Landon as to everyone else. "Traditional balls have connotations of being limited to heteronormative gender roles and relationships."

"Heteronormative?" asked Landon, looking back at her. "Do you mean normal?"

"There are no normal gender roles and relationships."

"There are in Louisiana."

"Normal changes," insisted Devorah. "Traditions die, including traditional gender roles and relationships."

"By traditional," asked Landon, "do you mean natural?"

"There are no natural gender roles and relationships."

"There are natural gender roles and relationships everywhere," insisted Landon, "even in New York, even if you can't see them anymore."

"Every aspect of the ball should recognize the diversity of gender," continued Devorah.

"We'll have diversity," said Landon. "There'll be boys and girls: the only decent kind of diversity. There'll be inclusion because they'll be dancing together: the only good inclusion. We don't want inclusion in the washrooms; that's creepy."

The challenge and confrontation might have come from only one person, but it was challenge and confrontation nevertheless. The meeting had become, in Landon's mind and it appeared in Devorah Chodorow's mind, a tussle between them. Whether the people sitting quietly adjudicated the outcome by their decisions about the ball, or a victor would emerge between Landon and Devorah Chodorow to which those other people would accede, remained to be revealed.

"There'll be equality," Landon told Devorah, "because

hopefully there'll be equal numbers of boys and girls, even if single boys and girls come alone hoping to get lucky. We'll have equal numbers of fathers and mothers in the Pavilion. Boys' and girls' tickets will cost the same: that's the only equality our boys and girls care about."

"Will they be blue tickets for boys and pink for girls?" asked Devorah.

"Good idea," retorted Landon, mocking her attempt at mocking him, "along with combination colors for joint tickets: one boy, one girl."

"What if two boys buy a ticket together, or two girls do?"

"They won't. Parents here raise their children well. I've only heard of boys liking girls and girls liking boys. I've only heard of boys and girls knowing what they are."

Devorah shook her head. "Three thousand people live in Garyville," she told him. (She must have checked that beforehand, thought Landon.) "Tens of thousands more boys and girls live around Garyville. I promise you: there are boys among them not liking girls and girls not liking boys. There are boys and girls exploring their gender options."

"Why do you promise that?" asked Landon. "Is it because it's true among three thousand boys and girls in your precinct in New York, or is it just a lie you tell to persuade people to your cause?"

"Do you want people to call you homophobic, transphobic, or bigoted?"

"They're bad and stupid words used by bad and stupid people to bully good and sensible people out of being good and sensible."

"You're a barbarian."

"The barbarians knew boys from girls and who each of them should like," retorted Landon. If he had ever cared what Devorah Chodorow thought of him, he had long stopped doing so. "They'd have recognized your sort for the deviants you are."

Devorah looked around the table. The submissive silence there continued.

Landon looked at the man who'd invited Devorah to the meeting. "Do you agree with all this, she's saying?" he asked the School Board representative.

"We agree with whatever will avoid controversy."

"People in Garyville would find her words and ideas more controversial than mine," answered Landon.

"We need to think of other people, too."

Devorah again spoke up. "We've become involved in cases on the basis of a single complaint."

Landon turned back to her. "All civil libertarians ever do is stop normal people from doing normal things," he told her. "You should change your name to civil despots."

From the sides of his eyes, Landon hoped to see someone around the table smile. Nobody did. They were probably too fearful.

"Diversity, inclusion, equality," insisted Devorah.

"Die," responded Landon.

"What?"

Landon explained. "Taking the first letters of the words 'diversity', 'inclusion', and 'equality' to form an acronym, as I know people from New York like to do, produces the word 'die'."

He knew she didn't see the fun of it. She didn't see the fun of anything. "That isn't being helpful," answered Devorah. "Wouldn't you like your ball to be a model for diversity, inclusion, and equality?"

"No. I want it to be enjoyable."

"People can still enjoy it."

"What joy is left after you gut it of frivolity, freedom, and fun?"

Devorah turned to the man who'd invited her, from the School Board. "Instead of a debutante ball," she told him, "call it simply a ball, or a dance. Avoid any gender representations in the promotional literature and tickets. State clearly that attendees are free to express their gender identities any way they choose. They may attend in whatever relationships they want."

Landon responded. "Seeing words like that would turn normal people off attending."

"I'd attend," said Devorah.

"You're not invited."

"If those words turn people off attending," continued Devorah, "then it's better they don't attend."

"What happened to your inclusion? Doesn't inclusion extend to normal people, with normal sensitivities?"

"You need to adapt."

"Why do we do all the adapting?" asked Landon. "You're not adapting."

She didn't answer him. He had been right.

The old restauranteur around the table spoke up, with his accent so Cajun even the Cajuns noticed it. "When people dink of Garyville, Louisiana," he said, "I want dem to think of the finest plantation home preserved as a museum in da South."

Everybody nodded, except Devorah. She might not have understood him.

"I don't want dem to think of controversies about dis dance. We have to dink of business."

The operator of the food mart chimed in. "I'm sorry, boy," he told Landon. "We've gotta agree with what she says."

Men and women around the table nodded, except Landon and Devorah. She had no need to nod.

"Friends," said Landon, implicitly if not explicitly excluding Devorah. "Are we again going to lose something worthwhile because one person, who isn't even one of us, objects? When do we start to tell those people to leave us alone? We're happy to leave them alone."

The old restauranteur answered him. "We'll say dat when other folks say dat," he said, "ones who visit New Orleans and want to take a breada and come to this ol' place." He looked around the Pavilion, although he surely meant the Plantation house outside. "Dey won't be at the ball, but dey'll be at this museum. Some o' dem will spend money in oda places. We can't afford to go out on our own, when no one else'll defend us."

Landon shook his head. "Who wants to buy tickets to a ball where they think they might see boys dressed as girls or girls dressed as boys?" he asked. "I know they won't, unless those people get wind of it from New York and come. I won't spend my time organizing a ball that doesn't celebrate my daughter's beauty."

"You're a sexist." Devorah told him.

Landon looked back at her, as he seemed forever to be doing. "I've been a sexist since before I knew there was such a word," he told her. "We all were, but I don't see a word as being a reason to stop knowing what I know to be true: what my wife, daughter, son, and I like being true."

The food mart operator addressed Landon. "We need you to be with us here, boy."

"If I am organizing it," said Landon, "then it's a debutante ball, for beautiful young women to showcase themselves to handsome young men showcasing themselves too. The young men and women won't be anything else."

Other than Landon and Devorah, the men and women around the table looked at each other. Some leant close to the people sitting beside them, to whisper something into their ears. Others stared, as if communicating by some secret message. Devorah watched Landon. Landon watched everyone.

The food mart operator broke the silence, speaking with a sad assurance in his voice. "There won't be a debutante ball in Garyville," he lamented, "not like the debutante balls Louisiana used to hold."

Any person wanting to counter that view had time to do so. Nobody did.

Landon stood up from his chair. He looked to the representative of the San Francisco Plantation. "We tried, Suellyn," he smiled. "I'm sorry, but thank you for hosting us today. Thank you for your time talking about this with me beforehand."

She smiled in return. "We try our best to accommodate our clients," she told him.

"You do," he said, "but some clients can't be accommodated."

Landon left the Pavilion. He returned to work.

By the time he returned home at the end of the day, his wife would have told their children there would be no ball, not in Garyville. None of them considered going to the ball in New Orleans; none of them felt confident to join that spectacle.

Seeing Trixie sitting in the swinging seat on the front porch, wearing an ordinary long dress, at least for her, Landon sat in a chair beside her. "You don't need fancy gowns for the world to see you're beautiful," he told her.

She looked at him. "Fancy gowns would be nice," she said. "Is this really me at my most appealing?"

He smiled. "You'll have times in your life to wear fancy gowns," he told her. "I have my times to wear my best dinner suit and hat."

She sighed. "Not often with me," she said. "I can't even tell you if Roscoe Jansen owns a suit and hat but, if he does own them, he's not worn them for me."

That seemed to be the end of it, until a Saturday evening a few weeks later. Landon was sitting in the living room of his home, drinking beer from a mug, dressed in ordinary home clothes, when the door opened to reveal Trixie. She stood glowing in a long shimmering silk white gown, revealing her smooth shoulders and uppermost suggestions of her cleavage, with her hair made up as if by a hairdresser preparing her for a ball.

Landon put down his mug and stood up. "You have grown up," he smiled.

"I ordered this when I thought there'd be a ball," she told him, stepping slightly into the room, twirling a little to show off the dress. "If I can't wear it with you giving me away, when will I wear it?"

"You will have a wedding day," Landon told her, "at the time and day you choose."

"Will I," she asked, "if you're the only man who sees me looking beautiful?"

Landon moved towards her. He prepared to hug her, when she pulled away.

"I can't have you ruining my dress," she told him. "If you want to make me feel better, you dress into the suit you would have worn for my debut."

If Trixie was being silly, she wasn't the only person to have been silly. Hers was, at least, a nice kind of silliness.

Landon left her there. He went upstairs, showered and shaved, as he didn't normally do a second time in a day. Finding his tuxedo and hat so rarely worn of late, he prepared himself in every way as he would have prepared himself for a debutante ball in Garyville: the ball that wouldn't be. Around his left wrist, he wrapped his gold watch. He folded a white handkerchief, which he carefully slipped into the breast pocket of his coat.

He always tried his utmost with what he knew and the resources available to him, but standing before the mirror, all he saw in the reflection was that unsightly birthmark on his cheek. He'd have covered it with his wife's make-up if he could, but all her skills with powder had never concealed it in the past.

In that reflection, he was hopelessly inadequate to have fathered the daughter waiting for him downstairs, but this was not the night to think of him. His daughter made him smile.

Careful not to trip in his best black leather shoes, Landon returned to the top of the stairs. At the foot of the stairs stood Trixie in her gown, looking up at him. Whatever they could do was lost to him, but she at least saw him at his insufficient best.

As he began down the stairs, Trixie addressed him. "I spoke to Suellyn at the San Francisco Plantation," she told him. "The Sugar

Mill Pavilion isn't being used tonight, so she said you and I can walk in there."

Landon laughed. "We should tell your mother and brother," he told her.

"I just did. They'll meet us there." Trixie's brother also owned a car.

A few decorative lights illuminated the San Francisco Plantation House, but inside was conspicuously dark. The Sugar Mill Pavilion had no lights, but for the headlights of Landon's car showing him the way.

Inside the Pavilion was dark. "The lights will come on," said Trixie, offering her father her hand.

"We should have music," said Landon, reaching out his bent elbow.

She rested her arm in his. "We are the music," she told him.

They stepped forward, the polished timber floor creaking with his heel and hers. Fathers were always slow to give their daughters away, but this would be particularly slow. Landon led them into darkness, as he'd always tried not to do.

The lights flickered on, including the scores of sparkling little lights stretched between the ceiling rafters. The Pavilion seemed bigger than it normally did, even when it was empty, but the Pavilion was not empty that night. Standing in the middle of the floor, dressed as if it were a ball, Landon's wife and son watched them. Similarly dressed were another young man and two people most certainly that young man's parents.

In a far corner of the Pavilion, watching without seeming to intrude, Suellyn Bonnier stood. In her long formal dress, she wasn't dressed as well as the other women there, but she was not there to impress.

They weren't watching Landon stepping forward. They watched Trixie, as they should.

Landon did not step quicker for the light. He might even have stepped slower. The evening had become one for all of them to savor.

When finally Landon and Trixie reached them, the unfamiliar young man stepped forward. "Good evening, Sir," he said to Landon, as nobody but sales assistants did. "My name is Roscoe Jansen. May I introduce you to my parents?"

Landon nodded, letting go of Trixie's arm. "This is my cue to step back," he told Trixie, for everyone to hear, "but never completely step back."

Roscoe led Trixie towards his parents. "May I introduce you to Miss Trixie Evans?"

They each made their introductions. Landon watched.

Roscoe took Trixie's arm, preparing to dance, before looking back at Landon. "Shouldn't we have music, Sir?" he asked.

"Wait," said Caleb, stepping away from the group. The group turned to face him, facing the door through which Landon and Trixie had come.

Standing at the door was another woman of about Landon's age, wearing what was surely her finest gown. All the women's hair had been carefully prepared, hours beforehand.

The woman stepped to the side. Entering the hall, also dressed for a ball, came a man of about Landon's age. Landon thought he recognized him from town, although never so well dressed in such a formal suit and hat as he was dressed that night. (Neither, for that matter, had Landon been so well dressed around the town, as he was dressed that night.) He led a young woman close to Trixie's age, her arm resting on his.

Her shimmering white gown shimmered a little differently to Trixie's shimmering white gown, accentuating her beauty no less than Trixie's gown accentuated hers, but this was not a time for parents to compare young women. Every woman making her debut was beautiful: all of them belles of the ball.

Among the five men now in the Pavilion, the suits and hats were much alike. Men's suits and hats were.

Much as Landon and Trixie walked, so that aging man and young woman walked. Her self-conscious smile would have been a giggle if she'd let it, but she was never going to let it. Her face became serious, focused on her steps head instead of the people to whom she headed.

When they reached Caleb, they stopped. Caleb stepped forward to face the older man. "Good evening, Sir," said Caleb, as Landon had never before heard his son address anyone, not even him. "My name is Caleb Evans." He pointed him to his parents. "May I introduce you to my parents?" He pointed them to Trixie. "May I introduce you to my sister, Trixie?"

Much as Landon had done, the aging man let go of the young woman's arm. Caleb took her arm, before turning to Landon and his wife. "May I introduce you to Amity Whest, who graciously invited me tonight?"

Landon nodded. Amity smiled a little more so.

Caleb led Amity a short way from the group, into an open space of floor, where they faced each other. His hand holding hers and one hand at her waist, she rested her hand on his shoulder. Roscoe and Trixie did the same, preparing to dance.

They were sights Landon couldn't previously have imagined seeing in his two children, not even through his planning for the debutante ball that was, after all. After the two young couples had enjoyed a dance or two, the three pairs of parents would dance with them.

At some point, Landon would invite Suellyn to dance. Each of the fathers would also invite her to dance, Landon felt certain, letting the mothers rest. The sons might invite her too, letting the daughters rest.

Before the young couples started to dance, Roscoe looked back at Landon. "Shouldn't we have music, Sir?" asked Roscoe.

Surveying his daughter with her bachelor, his son with his debutante, each couple ready to dance, a long broad grin rose though Landon's face and heart. He told the two young couples, for all their parents and Suellyn to hear, "You are the music."

6 THE NEW SCHOOL

Moving home can be difficult at any age, but there is probably no more difficult age to move than thirteen. Thirteen-year-old boys and girls are suddenly teenagers, a label that only reinforces their senses of no longer being children, without yet being adults.

The worst thing about moving home at any school age, when that move is of a sizeable enough distance, is moving school. The bigger the move, the worse it can be, especially when it crosses state lines. The more state lines it crosses, the bigger and worse it becomes.

Joey Noyce was thirteen, headed to Rhode Island because his father's employer had transferred his father there from its offices in Des Moines. Families followed employees.

More than most states appeared to people who'd not lived there, even if they'd visited, Rhode Island could intimidate. The smallest state in the Union, by area, it was also the second most densely populated, but it was the reputation of the rich in the Newport mansions and marinas that most unnerved Joey. He lacked personal experience to overcome those nerves, sitting in his family's Sport Utility Vehicle, headed eastward.

Every mile was little different from the last, even if Iowa and Rhode Island seemed so different, in first impressions. Iowa had space. Rhode Island did not, but still had more than the bulging cities between them.

According neatly, if coincidentally, with the Vanderbilt Hotel in which his parents, sister, and Joey lived while his parents found them a house to rent, or buy, Joey enrolled at Vanderbilt Middle School, eighth grade. If other boys and girls had reason to tease Joey for anything more than being a new student in school, then it would be his ginger hair, and the reddish tinge to his complexion that accompanied it. So he thought.

Teachers acknowledged the new boy in each class, but more briefly than new students had been introduced in Des Moines. New students might have been more common at Vanderbilt.

Nobody seemed to notice Joey's ginger hair. Nobody seemed to notice much at all.

At the mid-morning break that first day, Monday, standing at the lockers, several boys approached the new student. "I'm Sheldon," said one, "originally from Maine."

"I'm Quade," said another, "born in Boston." The children had already heard Joey's name in class. "Where are you from, Joey?"

"Des Moines."

"New Hampshire?"

"Iowa."

"Oh," said Quade. "I've never been west of New York."

"Why would you want to?" laughed a third boy, before looking at Joey. "I'm Reynold, only ever Rhode Island."

"I've been to Charleston," said Sheldon.

"Charleston, sure," said Quade, "and the Kentucky Derby, but only states that border oceans."

"Kentucky doesn't border an ocean," Joey corrected him.

"I know that!" insisted Quade, "but it's close to states that do, so it's like it does."

"Iowa borders Minnesota," said Joey, "but that didn't give us a border with Canada."

"You think you're smart," snapped Quade, "don't you, Joey? You're not. If you don't understand what I meant about Kentucky, then you're stupid!"

"I'm sorry," said Joey.

Quade turned to the other boys. "Let's leave him," he told them, "weirdo."

They left Joey alone, as he'd been before they approached him. Joey collected his books for the next classes.

The fourth period that day was Social Studies. Along with his introduction of Joey to the class, the teacher said to Joey, "I'm Mister Orford."

Mister Orford wore a beard, which at his young age was bright and brown. It made him seem modern, when beards on older men made them seem ancient. It also made him more memorable than the other teachers fronting Joey's classes that week. At the lunchtime recess afterwards, Reynold and Sheldon were much nicer to Joey without Quade around. "Mister Orford," said Sheldon, "he's the best."

Schoolteachers in Rhode Island seemed much like those in

Iowa, until the following Monday. At the Social Studies class that day, gone was Mister Orford's beard. Instead, he wore a wig of women's hair, in a fairer shade of brown than his beard had been and hair presumably remained, under the wig.

Gone was Mister Orford's shirt and trousers. In their place was a dark blouse and skirt. "I am Miss Orford, now," he told the class. "I've thought about this for a long time, and it's the right thing for me to do."

Joey had never before met people like Miss Orford, although he'd heard about them, as any American two decades into the twenty-first century couldn't help but hear about them. He'd only known people like Mister Orford.

Around Joey sat twenty-seven other boys and girls, sitting at their desks. Without expression, they looked at their teacher, as they'd looked at him through preceding classes.

None of them reacted. None of them laughed, or gasped. None of them shrieked, or cried, or left the classroom. One boy, Reynold, looked back at Joey.

With a tightening of his eyes and face, Joey tried to ask Reynold what was happening. Reynold didn't understand.

Mister Orford, or Miss Orford, proceeded to conduct the lesson as he'd conducted each of the lessons in which Joey had sat the preceding week. The boys and girls of the class, except Joey, sat, looked, and wrote as they previously had, continuing their routine. Only Joey looked around.

If those other boys and girls thought anything of Mister Orford, or Miss Orford, then Joey couldn't see it. Boys, girls, and even teachers couldn't hear each other's thoughts at the best of times. Just as well.

The view through the windows was unchanged from the preceding week. An obviously fantasy world outside that room would make the fantasy world inside the room seem reasonable, but even the weather outside was ordinary.

Perhaps Mister Orford was playing a prank on the new student from Des Moines? The other boys and girls must have all been party to the joke, so that soon they'd all leap from their chairs laughing at Joey's innocent expense; it would be better than them laughing at his ginger-colored hair. Mister Orford would also laugh, before whipping off his wig to reveal his hair.

His beard had gone. It was a shame about the beard.

Under his blouse and skirt, there probably wasn't room for Mister Orford's shirt and trousers. He could slip into his office to change his clothes.

Joey hadn't noticed whether Mister Orford carried a briefcase, suitcase, or satchel, in which he could have brought his normal clothes. On Mister Orford's desk was a handbag.

Stretching a little higher and to his side, Joey tried to see around Mister Orford's desk to see his shoes. He couldn't.

Joey never settled into the class. He looked at the writing book on his desk, opened only because opening it gave him something to do. He looked around the room at the other students more so than he looked again at Mister Orford – Miss Orford, whatever – standing at the front of the class. The teacher's voice remained as it had been the previous week, without playacting like a woman as his clothes playacted like a woman. Perhaps there, in that room of familiar children to whom he – she – was familiar, there wasn't any reason to falsify his voice.

If the change in circumstance played on Mister Orford's mind then it wasn't obvious. The manner of his teaching remained unchanged from one week earlier.

Joey closed his eyes. This was Mister Orford's Social Studies class. Nothing had changed.

"Joey!" Mister Orford's roaring voice – his masculine voice – interrupted Joey's thoughts.

Joey opened his eyes. Mister Orford was looking at him. Following Mister Orford's lead, other boys and girls were also looking at him.

"I'm sorry," said Joey, checking himself before saying "Sir," or "Ma'am." Joey had always told the truth, most of the time. He'd corrected people making mistakes, saying things he knew to be untrue, until that Social Studies class that day, but he'd never before heard a teacher say something so obviously untrue, as Mister Orford had.

Mister Orford resumed teaching his class. For all his concern about Joey closing his eyes, he remained unconcerned about Joey not writing anything as he spoke.

More discreetly than he'd previously been, Joey periodically looked around the classroom. Another child not writing was Sheldon, staring forward, down a little, with his eyes down further still. Sheldon too was distracted, his mind obviously in another place than the class in which they sat.

Leaving the classroom after the lesson, his books under his arm, Joey walked close to Reynold, carrying his books. "That was weird," said Joey.

"What?" asked Reynold, as they walked.

"Orford," answered Joey.

"What about her?"

"Her?" asked Joey, as he stopped walking.

Reynold also stopped. He turned to face Joey, while other students continued past them along the corridor.

"Don't you think it's weird?"

Reynold continued staring at Joey, until the long slow sense of recognition rose through his face. "We learnt about gender last year," he told Joey. "We saw some television shows, read a textbook. Miss Orford knows her gender better than we do."

"Didn't he know his gender last week?" asked Joey.

Reynold nodded. "She was mistaken then," he answered, without Mister Orford needing to have said so to his Social Studies class. "Now, she's discovered the truth."

"He's a man!" insisted Joey.

Reynold stepped close to Joey, forcing him towards the side of the corridor as Reynold looked around. "Don't let people hear you say that," he told Joey. "You'll get in more trouble than I can get you out of."

"Why?"

"She's Miss Orford and she's a woman," Reynold told him, "because she says she is. You'll find the same with boys and girls around the school discovering their genders, since we saw the television shows and read the textbook. If you say anything else, then you're not respecting them, and you don't want anyone to catch you not respecting someone."

Reynold turned and hurried along the corridor. Joey watched him go.

At the luncheon recess, Joey approached Sheldon, sitting quietly at a table, not eating anything. "You weren't paying attention in Social Studies," said Joey, sitting across the table from him. "Neither was I."

"I thought about Miss Orford," answered Sheldon, looking past Joey as if Joey wasn't there. "I should have been listening to the lesson, I know, but I think I'm the same."

"A girl?" asked Joey.

"I'll need a new name."

Joey shook his head. "When did you start thinking you're a girl?" he asked.

"I started wondering what gender I might be when we learnt about gender in class," answered Sheldon, of the time before Joey came. "When you hear about these other people and their experiences, you wonder about yourself."

"Do you believe everything you're taught in school?" asked Joey. "Don't you ever ask yourself, inside your head, whether teachers are telling you the truth?"

Sheldon set his eyes on Joey. "What we learn if we don't trust our textbooks?" asked Sheldon. "How can you expect to get satisfactory grades if you don't believe your teachers?"

Joey had no answer. He wanted to do well at school and he wanted to learn, but the two might not be synonymous. "You're a boy," Joey told him.

Sheldon stared at him. His face seemed to seize, a tear formed in his left eye. He stood up and rushed away.

Early that evening, Joey sat with his parents and younger sister on the deck of the Vanderbilt Hotel, in sight of the boats more numerous than any Joey had seen in Iowa, drinking glasses of iced water. "What do I say at school when people say things I know are untrue?" Joey asked his parents.

"Never say anything you know to be untrue," his father Bernard answered, as he had often said. "As for speaking up when other people say something you know to be untrue instead of politely keeping quiet: those decisions are part of growing up."

"How do you decide, Dad?"

Joey's father slowly sat more upright, adopting the stance of the sage whenever Joey invited his wisdom. "I think if telling the truth will hurt people," he told his son, "then remain silent, but if telling the truth will help them then, hard as it can be, I think you should speak up. Be polite, be courteous, but speak up nevertheless."

"What if I know the truth would help them, but they don't?" asked Joey. "What if telling the truth means they get upset and I get in trouble?"

His father sat silently, the sage in silence. Joey's eyes left his father again to look at the boats, their tall sails bobbing so gently as to be barely bobbing at all.

When they'd both spent too long in silence, Joey again spoke. "A week ago," he said, looking at the boats but talking to his father, "Mister Orford – I mentioned him to you – was a normal teacher." Joey looked from the boats back to his father, adjusting the focus in his eyes for the person close at hand. "Today, he comes into class dressed as a woman, saying he's a woman: Miss Orford."

Bernard looked at his wife. She shivered, as the wind from the water could do to a person. She looked away, leaving Bernard to answer.

He turned back to his son. "What did the other children say?" asked Bernard.

"Nothing," answered Joey. "If Mister Orford had come with his hair combed differently or wearing an unusually dark shirt, the boys and girls couldn't have said any less, except for my friend Sheldon; I think he's my friend. Sheldon would have wondered whether he too should comb his hair differently or wear a darker shirt."

The next day, Tuesday, was much like Monday had been, although Mister Orford didn't need to say what he'd said the previous day. Joey slowly adapted, listening to the teacher's words and taking notes as if Mister Orford still called himself Mister Orford, with his beard, shirt, and trousers. Sheldon appeared a bit distracted, but he and Joey didn't mention it during their conversations. They didn't mention Mister Orford or much else of anything.

In the evening, back at the Vanderbilt Hotel, Joey again sat with his family. This evening, they sat in a garden lounge, away from the sight of boats, where the air was a little less prone to the wind.

"Joey," said his father, "I spoke today with one of the Dads at the office about your problem. He said you've got to keep quiet if you can, but tell people you accept it if they ask. The boys and girls of your school will have learnt that from those gender lessons you mentioned."

Joey prepared to say nothing at school, but on Wednesday, Sheldon appeared at school in a dress. None of the boys or girls remarked upon it. None flinched or seemed to notice it, except Joey.

"Sheldon?" gasped Joey.

"Selena," replied Sheldon. "I'm Selena; I like the name Selena. I've told my Mom who's told the school to change its records. The teachers know to call me Selena."

For their core subjects, Sheldon and Joey sat in the same classes, with the same teachers. Their Language Arts teacher made no mention of Sheldon's new guise; she had no reason to do so. The Mathematics teacher mentioned Selena by name, when Joey thought he had no reason to do so. It was as if the teacher wanted to acknowledge Sheldon's new gender without drawing attention to it, as if there was nothing to which attention should be drawn.

Miss Orford paid attention. He, or she, wearing a wig and another new dress each day, stared at Sheldon, or Selena, wearing his or her first dress at school. They stared at each other without comment, before Miss Orford slowly embarked upon the lesson. She, or he, made no mention of Sheldon or Selena, as if neither of them were there.

That evening, sitting in their hotel room, Joey's father spoke of his day at his offices before Joey could speak of his day at school. "Somebody overheard me asking about people changing gender at work yesterday," Bernard told his family, his voice low and resigned. "The person complained to the human resources department that I was dismissing people discovering their gender. I had thought I hadn't said anything, or indicated my view one way or the other, but the person thought I was being dismissive. Now, tomorrow, I've got to explain myself before a company investigator."

"What will you say, darling?" Joey's mother asked him.

"I'll have to be respectful," answered Bernard. "I'll have to say I respect people's decisions about their gender, but I wanted to know the most respectful way to go about it. Whatever else I say, I'll keep talking about respect. It's what people want to hear, over and over. We don't have to respect them if we say we respect them, over and over."

Joey didn't mention Sheldon, or Selena, as he had planned to mention. He didn't want his father getting in any more trouble because of him.

The next day, Thursday, Selena wore the same dress he'd worn the previous day. "It's my sister's dress," he explained to Joey, without Joey having asked about it. "My Mom's going to take me to buy my own dresses this weekend."

"She doesn't mind?" asked Joey.

"She only wants me to be happy," said Selena. "She's my

friend."

"Isn't she supposed to be your mother?"

"She says she loves having another daughter. She's excited about it."

Joey could not imagine such a response from his mother. He could not imagine such a response from any mother, or father. "What does your Dad say?" asked Joey.

"He doesn't know," answered Selena. "I'm not due to visit him again until the end of the month."

Miss Orford, or Mister Orford, fronted their Social Studies class no longer wearing a dress or wig. He, or she, wore a baggy shirt and pants, dyed with swirling purple colors. His, or her, hair was short, as it had been, but unbrushed and uncombed. He, or she, was no longer apparently female. Nor was he, or she, obviously male.

"You should now refer to me as Mo Orford," he, or she, told the class. "I am neither male, nor female, but my own gender altogether."

Joey crashed his arms onto his desk. He crashed his head into his arms. "Oh, brother," he muttered, staring to the side.

He could have said "sister," Joey thought to himself. He probably should have said something else altogether, but Mo Orford hadn't told him what to say. To think, Joey thought to himself, two weeks earlier he'd worried about the reactions of other children to his ginger-colored hair.

The boys and girls he could see, standing on their sides because his head was lying down, stared back at him. No longer could Joey see Mo Orford, but he heard his teacher's voice: "Get me security."

Joey sat upright. Mo Orford was putting down a telephone that Joey hadn't heard being dialed, looking at Joey. The telephone call might have had nothing to do with Joey, although Joey felt certain it did.

Moments later, the classroom door opened. In came the School Resource Officer, wearing his distinctive dark-blue, short-sleeved shirt with its bright yellow badge and with a bevy of leather pouches around his waist, including a gun holster. Around his neck was a black cord holding a small radio and microphone, close to his mouth.

"Joey Noyce," Mo Orford told him, pointing the officer to Joey.

Still sitting at his desk, Joey watched the officer come towards him. He took Joey firmly by the top of his right arm, but not so firmly as to hurt him.

"Take your books, Joey Noyce," Mo Orford told him.

Joey did, gathering them under one arm, as the officer pulled his other arm upward, raising him from the chair. "Where am I going?" asked Joey.

"The principal," answered Mo Orford, "then a counselor, I expect. You should make sure that's the end of it."

Dragging Joey's arm, the School Resource Officer led Joey from the classroom and along the corridor. Joey headed with him along the next corridor, without thought of where he needed to head because the officer decided for him.

A girl at her locker watched him, rather than the officer, as they approached her part of the corridor. Their eyes met, Joey smiled, but she did not acknowledge him. She watched him as they passed.

She continued watching him. Joey turned his head to continue watching her, until he and the officer had gone so far past her that watching her became uncomfortable.

The officer led Joey up the stairs, to where the corridors were thinner. The door marked '*Principal*' was open. Through the door was a desk, at which sat a secretary on the telephone. She looked up to see the officer and Joey. "They're here, now," said the secretary, into the telephone.

Beyond her desk was a closed door, marked '*J Winkelmann.*' By the wall were several empty chairs. His hand still on Joey's arm, the officer sat with Joey in two adjoining chairs. Only then did he let go of Joey's right arm.

On Joey's lap, held by his arm, were his books. "Why am I here?" Joey asked the officer.

"That's not for me to say."

The secretary finished her telephone call. She left her desk, without looking at Joey or the officer, and went to the closed door. She knocked and entered what Joey could see past her was a private office, that of J Winkelmann, although Joey couldn't see J Winkelmann. The secretary closed the door behind her.

More so than at any other time in his life, more so even than the move from Iowa for his father's job, Joey sat powerless, dragged along by adults and their circumstances. Nominally, the officer was there because of Joey, as was probably the secretary in J

Winkelmann's office. In reality, Joey was there because of them: not them personally, or even Mo Orford personally, but because of the adult world to which he was expected to comply. The adult world did not seem very adult.

The principal's office door remained closed for several minutes, before opening again. The secretary reappeared, before closing the door behind her. "Take him to Ms. Kilpatrick," she told the officer, without ever looking at Joey.

The School Resource Officer again took Joey's arm, although Joey had learnt to stand before the officer stood. Less forcibly than he had been, the officer led Joey back to and along the corridor, to another open door. This door was marked '*Counselors.*'

Through the door were several more waiting chairs, although these were filled with children. Beyond them were several doors, all but one of which was closed. At the open door stood an older woman, older than Joey's mother, with longish gray hair and thin spectacles. She wore a beige blouse and cardigan, above a long beige woolen dress. She looked at Joey and smiled, before looking at the officer.

The officer led Joey to her. "We won't need you anymore," she told the officer, before looking at Joey. "Will we, Joey?"

She stepped back, inviting Joey through the door. He complied, whereby she followed him, closing the door behind them. Only she and Joey were in the room.

The room was like a small lounge room, with four orange vinyl chairs forming an uneven square. In the midst of them, but to the side so two chairs faced each other without interruption, was a low table. Standing on the table was a ceramic vase of artificial flowers.

Joey wondered how anyone could think those plastic flowers were real. He wondered whether anybody did.

In one of the two chairs facing each other, Ms. Kilpatrick sat down. Joey remained standing, facing her, until she waved her hand towards the chair. "Please, Joey," she said, "wouldn't you prefer to sit?"

Joey sat where she directed him to sit, adjusting himself several times trying to be comfortable, without ever being comfortable. On his lap, held by his arm, were his books.

"You don't need books," she told him, leaning forward. She took his books and placed them on the table. "Do you know why you're here, Joey?"

"Mo Orford sent me," said Joey.

Ms. Kilpatrick nodded. "I should have seen you earlier," she told him. "You were observed being disrespectful of Mo Ormond earlier this week."

"Who observed me?" asked Joey, looking around the room and up into the corners of the ceiling for surveillance cameras commonplace in corridors and other student areas, although he'd not thought they could hear students' voices. "That must have been when Mo Orford was Miss Orford."

"I don't know what you learned in Iowa," continued Ms. Kilpatrick, "but in Rhode Island, we respect people."

"We respected people in Iowa."

"When a person tells you his, or her, or any other gender, you must respect that person's knowledge. Why, I don't even like to refer to a person without first asking that person what gender that person is. How should I refer to you?"

"I've always been a boy," said Joey.

"Lovely," smiled Ms. Kilpatrick, "now I know."

"You didn't need to ask."

"But I did," insisted Ms. Kilpatrick. "What if I'd referred to you as being a boy but you knew yourself to be a girl? That would have been awful for you."

"It would have been dumb of me."

Ms. Kilpatrick leant forward in her chair. "Joey," she told him, "you're not dumb."

"I know."

"We're a community at Vanderbilt," said Ms. Kilpatrick. "Mo Ormond, the principal, your friend Selena, we all want you to feel free to find your gender. Nobody will pick on you, or bully you, or discriminate against you, whatever you tell us your gender happens to be."

"I'm a boy," said Joey, struggling to believe that he needed to say it.

"I respect that," said Ms. Kilpatrick, "but if you discover you're a girl, or non-binary, or any other gender, then I'll respect that to. Why, you might discover you're a gender I've never before heard. It might not even be a word, until you make it a word, and then it's a word and a gender as valid as any other. You have that right, and no other person has the right to question you."

Silence followed. If it was a silence in which Joey was supposed to discover his gender, he didn't need it.

"All we ask of our students, teachers, and everyone else," resumed Ms. Kilpatrick, "is that they respect the rights in others that they too enjoy. Is that too much to ask, Joey?"

Joey sat staring at her. If he was supposed to answer the question, then the answer was too complicated. The question was complicated, when it didn't need to be.

"When you slumped your hands and face into your desk in response to Mo Orford's announcement today," said Ms. Kilpatrick, "then you did not respect Mo Orford. Mo Orford felt disrespected by you. Now, Joey, is that fair to Mo Orford?"

There didn't seem to be anything for Joey to say, however much Ms. Kilpatrick would have wanted him to speak: to say he'd disrespected Mo Orford by slumping his arms onto his desk and head into his arms and would apologize to him. Joey would not say that. A week earlier, he'd respected Mister Orford, but he'd not respected Miss Orford and did not respect Mo Orford. Joey knew better than to say so, to anyone at school. "Why does Mo Orford care what I think?" asked Joey.

"I care what people think," said Ms. Kilpatrick. "I don't want them to be offended. Do you want people to feel offended?"

Joey looked around the room. It was a nice room, comfortable, if not for the conversation. He didn't care if people felt offended. They didn't care if he felt offended.

Ms. Kilpatrick drew a long sigh. "You know, Joey," she told him, "we can't have people being disrespected. Our students know that if they can't respect the genders of other people, without questioning them, or mocking them, then they need to stay at home until they learn respect. Do you want to stay at home, Joey?"

Joey didn't have a home. He had a bed at the Vanderbilt Hotel, lovely as it was, better than the home he'd had in Iowa, but not a home.

"Do you want the school to suspend you, Joey?" asked Ms. Kilpatrick. "With a telephone call, I can ask the School Resource Officer to escort you to your locker and from the school. We'll have some paperwork to complete and I'll need to inform your parents. Would you like me to ask them to come and sit with us now?"

Joey looked back at her. "No," he answered, for his parents' sake.

No matter how threatening her words, Ms. Kilpatrick's tone of voice remained soft and understanding. It also remained uncompromising. "If children can't appreciate gender diversity, Joey," she continued, "then we know they're very foolish, so we have to fail them in all their subjects, don't we, Joey?"

What Ms. Kilpatrick knew, Joey didn't. What Joey knew, Ms. Kilpatrick didn't, but Joey had no power to fail her. "I'll be more careful, now," said Joey. "I won't let Mo Orford feel disrespected, not by me."

Ms. Kilpatrick smiled. "Thank you, Joey," she said, offering him her hand to shake. "I think you can go back to your classes, do whatever Mo Orford asks of you, and we don't need to say anything more about it."

Joey shook her hand. She stood from her chair, as he reached towards the table and retrieved his books.

In the evening, Joey did not mention Mo Orford or the counselor to his parents. His father already had too much to say. "I am in a lot of trouble at work with this investigation," he told his family. "Don't ever say anything about people's gender, except to comply with everything they tell you."

Never had a weekend seemed so long coming as it seemed the next morning, Friday. That time seemed only longer when Joey saw Selena no longer wearing a dress. Instead, he, or she, wore a crumpled purple shirt and pants that could have been selected by Mo Orford.

Joey wasn't going to mention it. Selena did. "Yesterday afternoon, I realized I'm non-binary," said Selena. "This morning, I dressed for school expecting you to call me Mo, to refer to me as Mo, but entering the school, through the security checks, I wondered what Mo Orford might be. I realized I was waiting for him to lead me into telling me what I was, even if he didn't mean to lead me. I don't think he ever thinks of me."

Selena's change in pronouns was unmistakable, but Joey dare not mention it. He'd learnt that week not to say anything.

"I'm Sheldon. I'm a boy and I always was. Mom will tell the school today."

In one renegade moment, Joey wondered what corresponding realization Mo Orford might reach, but he couldn't speak aloud of such a possibility. Thoughts that might have risen in his head would only complicate his day, risking him saying words he couldn't say. Thus, Joey didn't think about them. He remained expressionless.

Within the week, the offices in Rhode Island dismissed Joey's father from his job. The company generously allowed him another chance at the offices in Des Moines, telling him it would be his last.

Joey's father drove their family in their Sport Utility Vehicle westward, back across state lines, with Joey again gazing into the passing scenery. Through the time of old America, people had known gender to be inescapable, without wanting to escape.

"I should say, Joey," said his father as he drove, "they'll be as crazy as New England soon enough in Iowa."

7 HANDBALL

Handball was a much less popular sport in America than it was in Europe, two decades into the twenty-first century, but still scattered around the country were handball courts indoors and out, including gymnasiums marked out and equipped to be courts. At the University of Virginia, the Slaughter Recreation Center wasn't named for the results of handball and other games convened there, although sometimes players felt it was.

Fewer even than the boys' handball teams in America were the girls' handball teams, like the team comprising high school girls from in and around Charlottesville. Whenever the requirements of the Cavalier Team Handball Club, not to mention other sports players and teams, allowed them, the girls took the court, or a just a corner, of the sprawling, shining Memorial Gymnasium. In one corner, the team would meet each Sunday morning through the season for training, before the game the following Saturday.

Coaching the team again was Erica Claridge, who'd recently graduated from the University but remained in Charlottesville to continue studying and work. Playing beach volleyball in Florida during breaks from college, Erica and other women had worn bikini tops and bottoms, but handball uniforms in Virginian weather were more modest shorts and jerseys. There were no earrings or other piercings, no necklaces or spectacles, all of which could injure a player or fellow player.

The first training session of the new season, beginning in the fall, Erica stood in her sweatshirt and tracksuit pants, with the team's kit bag on the floor beside her. She had expected to face twelve young women, aged sixteen or seventeen, dressed to play handball.

Eleven of the players standing before Erica that Sunday morning, looking back at her, were no surprise. Ponytails secured their fair or blonde hair from obstructing their vision in play. Their legs were long and sleek below their varied colored shorts no longer, or shorter, than any other girls' shorts; the team uniforms were only for games, beginning the next Saturday. In their hands, they held their pairs of gloves.

Standing amidst those eleven girls, as if the same as them, the twelfth person was nothing like that. The person was conspicuously taller than the other players, with broad arms and shoulders. Where girls had hips, the person did not, so that the person's shorts (longer and wider than other shorts there) hung loosely from a waist wider than all the other waists. The person's bobbed hair was thick, as was the person's head and neck.

Not that long ago, any Virginian handball coach, and indeed any coach of any team anywhere, would have assumed that the members of a girls sporting team were girls, but that was when biology determined gender and gender was less important than it had come to be, in America (and, for that matter, Europe). Like other American sporting associations, the handball association had announced that players could join the team of the gender by which they identified, although Erica had paid little thought to something so preposterous for her team, until that morning.

Erica stood staring at the person. The girls must have seen Erica staring, but to acknowledge her staring would have meant acknowledging the reason that she stared. None of them dared do that.

When she'd been at high school and even at University, Erica had been the same, but she was now well into her twenties. She'd moved away from childish things, when other Americans of her age she knew had not.

Only one name among the list of players Erica hadn't recognized from coaching the team the previous season; they'd all aged a year since then. "Are you Shannon Munzey?" Erica asked the unfamiliar person.

"I am," replied Shannon, in the softish, squeaky voice men used when trying to sound like women, without surgery to help them.

"You weren't part of our team last season?"

"I played in another team."

"Did you play in a boys' team?"

A girl in the team gasped. Another girl, standing beside Shannon where Erica easily saw her face, closed her eyes.

Shannon continued staring at Erica. "Why do you have to know?" asked Shannon, in a voice deeper than it had been. Shannon was forgetting to control it.

"I could ask your coach last year about your play," answered Erica, keeping her tone cordial. "I could ask about your strengths." Americans didn't like to speak of weaknesses any more: there were only strengths and areas to improve.

"I am the strongest girl on the team," said Shannon, "this team."

"Is that true?" asked Erica. "Is that fair?"

"Some people are stronger than others," persisted Shannon.

"Boys are stronger than girls," persisted Erica.

Again, a girl in the team gasped. The girl standing beside Shannon with her eyes closed still had her eyes closed.

"Not all boys," replied Shannon, "not all girls."

Erica thought carefully before responding, as she normally did. "Not all," she agreed, "but most."

A girl interrupted them. "Who will be captain this season, Erica?"

Shannon answered, "I want to be captain."

"Sloane Rutherford was captain last season," Erica told Shannon, as the girls on the team would have known.

"She shouldn't be captain again," insisted Shannon. "We should give another girl a chance."

Shannon had a point, Erica understood. "Sloane was a very good captain last season," Erica told them all, especially Sloane, looking around at each of the girls in turn, "but would another girl like to be captain this year?"

"I would," Shannon said again.

"We should see if anyone else would like a chance," said Erica. "The girls played as a team last year."

"I'm a girl," insisted Shannon.

Erica knew better than to answer Shannon. Instead, she set her eyes upon Ann-Marie Whittaker. "Ann-Marie," said Erica, "you also wanted to be captain last season, when I chose Sloane. Would you like to be captain this season?"

"That isn't fair," interjected Shannon.

Erica continued facing Ann-Marie, who remained uncharacteristically silent. "Ann-Marie?" asked Erica.

Again, Shannon interjected. "Why should what she said last season mean anything now?" asked Shannon.

Ann-Marie remained silent. Hers was the silence of discretion, knew Erica, fearful of denying Shannon as she would not hesitate denying a girl to get something she wanted. Erica knew Ann-Marie well enough to know she would still like to be captain; choosing Sloane last season had been a difficult choice. More importantly, Ann-Marie had the respect of the other girls, including Sloane. Most importantly, Erica was not so willing to accommodate Shannon Munzey as the high school girls were. "Ann-Marie," said Erica, "you can be captain this season."

Shannon again interjected. "She never said she wanted to be captain this season," Shannon told Erica. "I did."

Surprised to be called upon to justify her decision, Erica turned her head to Shannon. "The girls know Ann-Marie," said Erica.

"I'm a girl," Shannon said again. "I don't know her."

"The other players know her."

The training session had again become a confrontation between Erica and Shannon. "We should have a vote," demanded Shannon, strangely oblivious, thought Erica, to what the outcome of that vote would be. Slowly, Erica realized that Shannon knew the girls dare not deny Shannon anything.

A girl in the team interrupted. "Can we please play handball?" she asked, a little rudely. "Can we practice, if we're not going to be coached?"

"So sorry," said Erica. "Of course we can. Shall we loosen our sporty muscles?"

Shannon continued standing, while the girls stepped back and to their sides, spreading around into small spaces in their corner of the gymnasium floor, leaving Shannon alone. With Erica leading, the girls exercised, limbering their arms and hands, their legs and ankles, their necks and backs. Slowly, Shannon repeated the exercises.

Watching each team member in turn, Erica saw the clumsiness in Shannon, the beefiness. The girls appeared graceful, as they never had before Shannon came. That was something more for Erica not to say.

"We'll practice throwing and catching," said Erica.

Donning their gloves, the girls formed rows along each side of the court, spaced apart so they faced each other in pairs. The side without Shannon clustered awkwardly, so that nobody faced Shannon, ball in glove.

Practice was the time to test the players, and the best of the players the previous season had become the captain for the new.

"Ann-Marie," said Erica, "you throw with Shannon."

For a moment, Ann-Marie stood staring at Erica, while the other girls reconfigured into pairs, passing balls around so one girl in each pair of girls held a ball. Reluctantly, Ann-Marie stepped to where she faced Shannon. Erica stepped back, out of everybody's way.

Shannon threw the ball hard at Ann-Marie, who missed catching it altogether. The girls often did at practice.

While other girls threw balls between themselves, sometimes leaping, occasionally not catching, Ann-Marie recovered the distant ball she'd missed. She returned to her place in the line, and threw the ball at Shannon as hard as she could. Shannon caught the ball effortlessly, before promptly throwing it back harder than the first time at Ann-Marie.

The ball struck Ann-Marie's gloved hand more than Ann-Marie almost caught it, before spearing onwards. Her other hand held that hand, while slowly she ambled across the floor towards the ball.

"We'll try some exercises," said Erica.

The two lines dissipated, as the players spread evenly around their portion of the court. Erica guided them through familiar steps and moves, holding balls in their hands and handling balls while keeping balance. Ordinarily, Erica would have let pairs of players, or sometimes groups of three, compete with each other around corners of the court, or separate the team into equal sides to play the other. That morning, she kept the players on their own, separate from each other and the burly Shannon Munzey.

Erica could keep Shannon apart from the girls during practice. She couldn't keep Shannon apart from the girls of Erica's team, or the opposing team, at the game the coming Saturday.

Towards the end of the time allotted for practice, the players again stood around Erica. "Can Shannon be the goalie?" one girl, who'd been the goalkeeper the previous season, asked Erica. She held the goalkeeper jersey in her hand, ready to give away.

The goalkeeper was the player most important in preventing the opposing team from scoring a goal, but might also be the player least likely to barge into other players. Most interestingly, thought Erica, masculine anatomy required male goalkeepers to wear physical protection from particular injuries to which female anatomy was not susceptible. "Our team doesn't have a jockstrap," said Erica.

"Ah," gasped a girl in the team. Whether the same girl or different girls did all the gasping, Erica couldn't tell.

"I never thought we'd need it," Erica added, unnecessarily.

Shannon responded. "I don't want to be goalie," said Shannon. "I want to move around the court. I want to be in the action."

"I can't have you crashing into girls," said Erica.

"I am a girl," insisted Shannon, yet again.

"Goalies are normally the biggest players on a team," Erica told Shannon. "You are the tallest on this team, the biggest, by a long shot. I'm certain you'll be the tallest and biggest on the court this Saturday." For good measure, and for the fun of it, she then added: "You might be the tallest and the biggest in the whole gymnasium."

"I don't want to be goalie," Shannon said again. "I won't be goalie."

"You will be goalie," insisted Erica, before offering a consolation she had no intention of implementing. "We can change goalie through the game."

Turning heads, with some girls starting to step away, drew Erica's attention to the mothers and fathers, some with siblings, some with step-parents, appearing at the gymnasium doors to collect the players. The players rarely showered at the gymnasium after practice, but often did after games, especially those games to which they'd travelled far from home.

Erica hadn't noticed Shannon entering a washroom that morning to know which washroom Shannon used, although Erica could have guessed. (If men and women sharing washrooms did anyone a favor, it was someone like Shannon Munzey.)

Showers were more problematic. Before that day, Erica hadn't thought to notice players using showers, any more than she'd noticed players using washrooms.

"Shannon," said Erica. Shannon faced her. "Can you stay behind for a moment?"

Those words made Erica feel like a schoolmistress, much older than she was. The girls moved towards their families, leaving Shannon and Erica alone.

"After games," said Erica, "after practice, if you want to shower, are you planning to enter the female bathrooms and showers?"

"Why wouldn't I?" asked Shannon.

"I've got fathers, and mothers, who won't want you so close to their daughters."

"You're so cruel."

"You're being cruel," said Erica, "expecting people to indulge you while you won't accommodate anyone else."

"Are you a Christian?" asked Shannon.

Erica hadn't expected Shannon to make their conversation about her. "Not with the parties I've attended," answered Erica, "since you ask."

"I'd expect your sort of attitude from Christians."

Erica laughed, at the expense of some of the Christians on campus. "You'd be surprised," she answered. "I'm thinking of the girls."

"I am a girl!" Shannon said again, clenching his fists and pounding them in the air. "I am a girl! I am a girl! I am a girl!"

Erica thought of saying she didn't need to keep declaring her gender, as Shannon needed to keep declaring his, or what wasn't his. She thought better of it.

His fists still clenched, Shannon turned and stormed away, his sturdy frame and thick legs set headstrong towards the open gymnasium door. Erica watched Shannon go to a woman (Erica thought she was a woman) old enough to be Shannon's mother, standing waiting by the door. Perhaps she was Shannon's mother, to see her step towards him and put her arm around him, as best as she could with him so much taller and bigger than she was. Shannon's head dipped forward, but Erica from behind could not see Shannon's face to know if he was crying. The woman and Shannon went out through the open door together.

The game that coming Saturday was a problem about which Erica could not do anything, except be ready on the day for anything to happen. There was no point in her worrying about it until then, she thought.

That was until a day later, Monday, when Erica received a telephone call from Dimity Guffle, of the Cavalier Team Handball Club. Erica agreed to meet with her, although Dimity suggested Erica not come back to the University grounds, not until after they'd spoken. Instead, they met soon after one o'clock in the atrium of the Omni Hotel.

Erica arrived first, to where the palm leaves in a bright space were an opportune distraction from everything outside. Taking a seat along the cushioned lounge at an empty table left a less comfortable empty chair for Dimity to occupy, when she arrived soon afterwards.

Dimity was still a student at the University, but she and Erica had previously met at handball games and parties. She brought a small packet of chewing gum from her handbag and offered Erica a stick, but Erica shook her head. Dimity removed a stick, unwrapped it, and folded the gum into her mouth.

"Erica," said Dimity, chewing her gum. "Shannon Munzey's mother says you're picking on her."

"In what way?" asked Erica. Asking a question seemed her best response, at least initially.

"She says you stopped her from being team captain," said Dimity. "She says you're forcing her to be goalie when she doesn't want to be goalie."

Erica wasn't going to use a pronoun she knew was untrue, however often Dimity did. "Being new to the team," said Erica, "Shannon isn't qualified to be captain." If Erica knew Shannon's name before he called himself a girl, she would have used it. "Being the biggest and strongest player, Shannon is suited to being goalkeeper."

"We need to be tolerant," insisted Dimity, chewing her gum.

Erica had never before suffered a conversation like their conversation that day. "Shannon Munzey doesn't tolerate anybody else," she said.

"We need to try to make things easier for her."

"Why?" asked Erica. "Have you noticed that we only see men forcing their way into women's sports, with their physical advantages? Third-rate male athletes become champions by calling themselves women and playing in women's sports; how do we know that's not what Shannon's doing with his handball? We don't see women, however talented or talentless we are, demanding a right to play men's sports, where we physically haven't got a chance."

Dimity continued staring, chewing her gum, until Erica was silent for long enough for Dimity to know she'd finished. "As far as you," said Dimity, momentarily not chewing, "I, and this club and university are concerned, Shannon Munzey is a girl."

All the passion was Erica's. "We're not doing Shannon any

favors by indulging his delusion," said Erica, "or his lie, if that's what it is. He's not going to get any counselling or other psychological assistance if we all tell him he doesn't need it. He's not going to tell the truth if we're no less dishonest than he is."

"It's not up to you, or me, or anyone else but Shannon, to decide what's right for Shannon."

"Why isn't it up to me, you, and all of us?" asked Erica. "I'd want you or someone else to tell me if I was being so terribly, terribly stupid."

"That's Shannon's right," insisted Dimity. "You're not going to change that."

Erica looked down at the table; no answers came to her. "Don't the girls playing handball have rights?" she asked, without looking up.

"The girls aren't the problem," answered Dimity. "Shannon's mother says that you're the only problem."

Erica looked up again at Dimity, chewing her gum. "I'm not going to punish Ann-Marie Whittaker by denying her the captaincy," said Erica. "You will have met Ann-Marie..."

"Ann-Marie won't object to Shannon Munzey being captain," insisted Dimity, presumably with less knowledge of Ann-Marie in particular than of all high school boys and girls. "She's not going to want Shannon's mother complaining about her the way Shannon's mother is complaining about you."

"Ann-Marie shouldn't be put in that position," said Erica. "You and I need to think of her and we need to think of the team."

"If we leave Shannon feeling she's been picked upon," insisted Dimity, as if Shannon Munzey feeling picked upon meant that Shannon Munzey was being picked upon, "then the Cavalier Team Handball Club and the University of Virginia will withdraw permission for your team to play."

"That isn't fair on the team," complained Erica.

"I also want you to choose another goalkeeper."

"Have you seen Shannon Munzey?" asked Erica.

"I've only spoken with her mother."

"If Shannon's allowed to bundle around that court, he'll crash into the girls and injure them. Do you want them or their families suing you for the injuries?"

"Handball is a competitive game," said Dimity. "It's a contact sport, and players know the risks every time they step onto the court."

"Girls don't know the risk of Shannon Munzey," insisted Erica. "Boys know, but not girls."

"There are some strong and heavy girls," said Dimity.

"Girls aren't as strong and heavy as Shannon Munzey, not in handball."

Dimity looked around the atrium, as if to tell Erica that she had nothing more to say. Intentionally or otherwise, that gave Erica time to think: time to think of anything less than giving Shannon Munzey everything he wanted. Refusing to indulge him was Erica's responsibility, even if she was the only person in Charlottesville to see it.

"I'll make Shannon Munzey captain," surrendered Erica, drawing Dimity's attention back to her. "I'll tell Ann-Marie that Shannon's mother complained to you that I was persecuting Shannon and we have no choice but to make Shannon captain. You can tell Shannon's mother that you've given her what she wanted."

If Ann-Marie and other girls hated Shannon Munzey, then that was not Erica's concern. She wasn't going to protect Shannon Munzey from blame, at her or anyone else's expense. Besides, she did not think the girls would blame Shannon. They'd been taught too well to indulge people like Shannon Munzey to deny them anything, so would tolerate Shannon costing Ann-Marie the captaincy as they would not tolerate Erica or anybody else doing so.

Dimity nodded. "You could put Ann-Marie in goal," she told Erica.

Erica shook her head. "Ann-Marie is too thin to be in goal," she said. "In return for making Shannon Munzey captain, I want Shannon to stay in goal, away from other players. We can say it's the best place to be captain, looking down the court, whatever other people say, whatever you and I might know. I'll put up with Ann-Marie's injured feelings about the captaincy before I put up with any of the girls, or any girls from other teams, being injured physically. Shannon Munzey is big enough to kill some of these girls, however inadvertently."

Dimity sat silently, presumably contemplating Erica's proposal. It was a compromise more generous to Shannon Munzey and less sensitive to Ann-Marie and the interests of the team than Erica wanted to be, but Erica could not do any better.

The gum that Dimity chewed had surely, thought Erica, long run out of flavor, but never seemed to end. Finally, Dimity spoke. "I'll tell Shannon's mother of your proposal," she said. "If she accepts it, and if Shannon accepts it, then the Club and University will accept it, but if either of them don't, then we will stop your team from using the Club and University facilities until you choose another goalie, keeping Shannon Munzey captain. You might find another gymnasium in Charlottesville to host you, but I don't think so. I think Shannon's mother will make certain you don't."

Erica nodded. "You're probably right," she smiled, "but shutting down the team and all the girls suffering that disappointment is better than them being barreled over by Shannon Munzey."

Dimity rose from her chair and the table, removing her gum from the side of her mouth and slipping it into its wrapper she must have been holding in her hand. "I'll call you if there's a problem," she told Erica, before smiling. "Good luck with the game on Saturday."

Erica did not hear back from Dimity. Thursday evening, she telephoned Ann-Marie to tell her of her meeting with Dimity: that Shannon's mother's complaint to the University and Club meant Ann-Marie had lost the team captaincy to Shannon.

Ann-Marie softly sighed, but did not say anything that anyone could construe as a complaint. She knew better than that.

That coming Saturday morning, the team was playing a team of high school girls from around Chapel Hill, who utilized a court at the University of North Carolina much as Erica's team borrowed theirs at the University of Virginia. Last time they'd played, last season, in North Carolina, the contest was tight, before the North Carolinians won by a single goal.

This time, they played at the University of Virginia, back in the Memorial Gymnasium of the Slaughter Recreation Center. From the rows of chairs at the side of the court, mothers and sisters, with a few fathers and brothers, from both teams sat ready to watch the game.

Dressed in their team uniforms, the players readied themselves. Shannon wasn't wearing the distinctive goalkeeper's jersey; goalkeepers were no longer compelled to wear them, although many did. Embarrassed to be looking, but careful not to let anybody see that she was looking, Erica tried to see if Shannon wore a jockstrap in his shorts. She didn't think so, but wasn't certain. She knew she couldn't ask.

When the players used the bathroom before the game, Erica paid particular attention to Shannon's choice of bathroom. Shannon entered the women's bathroom.

From a distance, Erica watched and listened. No sound of commotion or anything else came from the bathroom. A couple of girls leaving the bathroom looked at each other as they did, without speaking that Erica heard. Soon, quite soon, Shannon left the bathroom. Erica looked another way.

The players standing together, Erica addressed them. "You recall your opposition from last season," she said, before looking at Shannon, "except you, Shannon." Erica looked back at the girls. "They'll remember you, I'm positive, but they won't remember Shannon."

Some of the girls smiled. Shannon's face remained serious, more intense than other faces. If any girls of the opposing team said anything of the player so much bigger than any other on either team, Erica couldn't hear them.

The game beginning, Erica and the opposing coach stepped back to the sides of the court. Six of the girls from each team took their field positions on the court. Shannon stood in one goal, facing the field of play.

Goalkeepers normally remained close to the goals they defended, except in the last minutes of a close game when they might risk everything and join their teammates around the court to improve their chances for a goal. The rules of the game allowed them to do so, provided they weren't carrying or dribbling the ball. Never had Erica seen a goalkeeper leave the goal at the beginning of a game, until the start of that game. Shannon immediately rushed headlong into the field of play.

Some players from Erica's team looked to her as if to ask what Shannon was doing. Erica shook her head; she didn't know. She thought of calling Shannon back to the goal perimeter, but there wouldn't be any point. Shannon appeared to have agreed to be goalkeeper without any intention of being goalkeeper. Nobody told Shannon what he was. Nobody told him what to do.

After a moment or two, it seemed the players had taken stock of Shannon's action. Ann-Marie moved to the goal perimeter, effectively becoming goalkeeper.

Meanwhile, Shannon told girls to get out of his way as he chased the ball. He was often at the ball, pushing aside girls from his team as freely as he pushed aside girls from the other team, taking the ball, sometimes leaping, and throwing it goalward, without thought of passing it to his teammates. When his aim was poor, he told his teammates to catch the ball, without mentioning the girls' names he probably didn't know. They often dropped the ball, but when they caught it, collected it, or otherwise took hold of it, Shannon told them to throw it back to him, rushing through the court.

One girl from the other team pushed aside by Shannon fell to the floor. Another player from her team went to her, helping her stand. The play continued.

Bounding quicker to the ball than the girls could, Shannon was everywhere. It seemed every second person to take the ball was Shannon, leaping with the throw and running to challenge whatever girl then caught it, or went after it. Grappling for the ball, Shannon again knocked over a girl from the opposing team. The girl crashed to the floor. She burst into tears.

The referees stopped play, as a woman from among the spectators rose from her chair. One of the second fallen girl's teammates and then another helped her stand. She hobbled a little as she left the court, with two teammates and then a third. Another player from her team entered the court, but the players from the opposing team had gathered with their coach at a side of the court.

The two referees stood talking with each other. Parents of players in both teams were leaving their chairs, to stand near their girls at a side of the court.

Without the opposing team at play, a member of Erica's team approached her. "I'm not getting a go," she complained. "None of us are, except Shannon."

"So sorry," said Erica. "I'd do something if I could."

The girl looked at Erica, as another of Erica's charges stood beside her. "I'm going home," she said. She walked to her parents coming towards her. Together they left.

A mother approached Erica, and then another. "Can you do anything to help?" one asked. "The girls love their handball."

"We've all paid our registration fees," said the other mother. "Our girls aren't getting to play."

"I tried to say something," said Erica, shaking her head, pleading for understanding, "but it didn't help. There's nothing I can do."

"I don't think we'll be back," said the first mother, taking her daughter away.

"We'll look for some other activity," said the second mother. She and her daughter also departed.

Leaving her girls and their families gathered together, the coach of the North Carolinian team approached Erica. "We're forfeiting the game," she told Erica. "You've won. You've won every game our team's playing against yours."

"We haven't won," lamented Erica. "We won't win."

The forfeiting coach returned to her team. The forfeiting team and their families departed.

The girls of Erica's team and their families departed, some mothers and daughters telling Erica that their daughters would find other things to do; one might try volleyball, another lacrosse. Those that didn't tell Erica didn't need to.

Finally, only Shannon remained with Erica, standing on the court. The only spectator left in the rows of chairs was the woman presumably Shannon's mother, watching Erica and Shannon. Erica began collecting the team handballs and other materials into the team kit bag.

"I want to play," said Shannon. The voice was male, no longer mimicking a female voice as best he could, at least that morning.

Erica turned towards her. "Your only thoughts are about you, aren't they, Shannon?" said Erica.

Shannon stared at her, before calmly saying again: "I want to play."

"I can't coach a team of one, Shannon," said Erica. "One person can't be a team."

Shannon's mother came across the floor towards him. She put her arms around him. "Now, now, bumpkin," she said, before looking at Erica. "Will you find us more players?" she asked, the two of them facing Erica.

Erica shook her head. "Would Shannon like to try golf?" she asked, not entirely flippantly.

"I want to play handball," said Shannon.

"She wants to play handball," Shannon's mother repeated, although there was hardly any need to do so.

"I can't pull players out of the air," pleaded Erica.

"I think you could have done something to help," replied Shannon's mother, "instead of turning the other girls against her. This isn't fair on Shannon."

Erica resumed collecting everything into her kit bag, Shannon and his mother watching her. Picking up the kit bag, Erica began to walk away. Behind her, she again heard Shannon telling her, "I want to play."

She didn't answer. Erica continued walking, towards the gymnasium door.

Her steps prevented Erica from hearing whether Shannon and his mother behind her were also leaving. Louder this time, Shannon called out, "I want to play."

8 KIRK AND ISLA

"Do we agree about everything?" Kirk Hartley asked his girlfriend Isla Peale, amidst another conversation between them about matters material and not.

"No," she answered.

"What?" checked Kirk, moving closer to her. "What don't we agree about?"

"That we agree about everything."

Trying to fathom her reply, Kirk stared at her deep brown eyes, but staring there distracted him from thinking about anything but her; his reflection in those eyes could seem blessed for being reflected there. Those eyes began to smile and laugh as the rest of her face smiled and laughed. Kirk laughed with her, grabbing her thin waist and kissing her again.

Wearing her tall shoes, they were about the same height, which made kissing her easier than kissing other women had been; Kirk was a little taller than most men, and at twenty-three years of age wasn't going to grow any taller. Yet Isla was light to hold, moving with every motion Kirk made with her, before she rested her arms around his chest, broadening it still more.

Their kiss was long, as their kisses always were but never long enough. It ended for the same reason their kisses normally ended: for Kirk to see her face and the rest of her again.

With her long waving brown hair and face uncommonly delicate, Isla could have modelled swimsuits and other womenswear, Kirk often told her. In response, she'd giggle, before shaking her head. He'd then kiss her again.

Kirk's time to be with her would soon finish as it finished every Saturday at about that time. Isla worked in a pottery store along State Circle, the sometimes quiet one-way street around the park of the Maryland State House: a state house as elegant as any but quieter than most, because historical Annapolis was quieter than most state capitals.

Meeting for lunch was more difficult through the normal

working week. Kirk's was a usual Monday-to-Friday job in the administrative offices of the United States Naval Academy. With Isla working Saturdays, and sometimes Sundays, Saturday lunchtimes meant more to Kirk than they did to most people, although he and Isla had evenings and most Sundays together.

At the end of Isla's time for lunch each Saturday, after they'd eaten or just been together, Kirk walked with her back to the pottery store doors. They kissed a final time, although they'd kiss again many times that evening, before she climbed the two stone steps back into the store. Her long arm to her hand held his, almost dragging him into the store as he almost kept her outside, before she stepped away.

From the sidewalk, Kirk would watch her in the store, until a shopper entering the store or leaving necessitated him stepping to the side. If the day was warm enough, a door from the store remained open. If it was cold, then the doors would be closed, but the glass panes in the doors, like those in the windows, were always clean. He'd then wonder what to do through the afternoon, before meeting Isla outside the store after it closed.

That Saturday, still watching her from the sidewalk through the open door, about to start wondering, a man's voice interrupted Kirk's routine. "What do you know about Isla Peale?" asked the voice.

Kirk turned to see a young navy cadet in profile, looking through the glass into the store. His uniform was immaculate and hair cropped short as navy men wore it. Working in the administrative section, Kirk's hair wasn't quite that short. Kirk's shirt and trousers weren't a uniform and certainly weren't immaculate.

"Do I know you?" asked Kirk.

"I saw you kissing," he answered, turning towards Kirk. "I'm Travis. I used to date Isla."

"She hasn't mentioned you," said Kirk, before adding words to make his response more about Travis than about him. "She has told me she had boyfriends before me."

"What else has she told you about her?"

"She's told me enough."

"How do you know?"

"Why are we having this conversation?" asked Kirk. "I don't mean to be rude, but I've broken up with girlfriends. I know it hurts, but I move on. When I'm happy with the girlfriend I've got, I'm glad to have split from the others. You should be too."

"I am happy," said Travis. "I'm engaged to be married, to a beautiful girl from South Dakota; she makes me happy. I'm from North Dakota originally, before joining the Academy, so we see the world from much the same place, but you don't want too much in common. I had too much in common with Isla, way too much. My fiancée and I, we're planning a family."

"Why aren't you with your fiancée now?" asked Kirk.

"We were wandering together, much as I used to wander with Isla, when I saw you and Isla together; Isla didn't see me. My fiancée already knew about Isla, but this was the first time she saw her. I told her I wanted to speak with you and the reason I did, so she said she better leave."

"So had I," said Kirk, turning his back to Travis and walking away. He turned into Francis Street, down the hill towards the harbor.

Soon, Travis was walking with him. "Do you know how much you've got in common with Isla?" asked Travis.

Kirk stopped to face him. "I like having a lot in common with my girl," Kirk told him. "She likes it; we can't have too much in common. Maybe she dumped you because she wanted her man to be more like her."

Travis laughed. "She wanted to be less like me," he said. "I split from her; it was my decision."

"Then you should have got over her real quick."

"I didn't," said Travis. "I felt sick for having gone out with her. I felt sick for having touched her, for kissing her, for… Well, you can imagine."

"Aren't Navy people tougher than that?" asked Kirk.

"We're tough about most things," replied Travis, "but not about everything. Nobody is."

"If I saw my ex-girlfriend with a new fella," said Kirk, "I wouldn't approach him the way you approached me. I might talk to her with him, if they walked towards me and talking to them was more mannerly than looking the other way. I might say something brief but nice to him, to be polite without intruding, without a conversation like the one you're having here with me."

"I'm trying to help you," said Travis.

"Why not help Isla?"

"I'd love to help Isla, but Isla knows enough to help herself. You don't."

Kirk again turned back down the hill. "Good day, Travis," he said, stepping forward. "I'll tell Isla I met you."

"What has Isla told you about her childhood?" asked Travis.

Kirk again stopped, without turning back to Travis. He sighed, more audibly than he needed to be.

"Has she shown you any photographs from her childhood?" asked Travis.

She hadn't. They weren't important. "Here and now is important," said Kirk, still looking down the hill. "The future is important."

"Do you want to have kids?" persisted Travis.

Kirk turned around, stepping a little closer to Travis. "That's a conversation for me and Isla."

"Have you had that conversation?" asked Travis. "Isla and I did; she's a few years older than I am so I thought we should."

Twenty-three years of age wasn't old, thought Kirk, but he too was twenty-three years old. Travis was younger.

"She told me she wanted kids," continued Travis. "Only later did I learn she meant she'd adopt, but adopting kids isn't having kids, is it?"

It wasn't, but Kirk didn't need to say so to Travis. "Where's this going, Travis?"

"Ask to see her childhood photographs," said Travis. "She doesn't have any; she destroyed them."

"What are old photographs going to teach me that seeing her in front of me won't?" asked Kirk. "That's what I want to see: the woman, not the girl. What's wrong with you?"

"Ask to see her high school yearbook. She doesn't have that. Ask to catch up to her high school friends. She'll say that's a good idea, but you never will. Has she mentioned her mother and sisters?"

"I know they live in Denver."

"Tell her you want to meet them. Get in your car and tell her you want to drive there now, or tell her you've bought plane tickets or bus tickets for you both to go there and see what she says. I promise you, you'll never get her to Denver. They'll never visit you; I doubt they know where she lives. It's as if she didn't exist a year ago. Don't you want to know why?"

Kirk opened his hands in the air, shaking his head. "If it was important, she'd tell me."

"It is important," said Travis. "I think it's important, and when you know the reason she's buried her past where no one can see it, not even her, you'll think it's important. I know there are people who don't think it's important, she told me she's one of them but she would. I don't think you're one of those people."

Kirk thought of asking him what he was talking about, but that was a question for Isla, if it was a question for anyone. It probably wasn't.

"Is she working tomorrow?" asked Travis. "She used to work some Sundays. I don't think the potters of the store know anything about her."

"Goodbye, Travis," said Kirk, again turning to leave.

"Three o'clock, tomorrow afternoon," said Travis, "I'll be by the Kunta Kinte Memorial on the wharf." The memorial was well known to everyone in Annapolis.

Kirk turned back to him. "I thought you boys worked hard?" said Kirk. "I thought you studied every night and weekend?"

"The wharf reminds me why I want to be in the navy," explained Travis, "not just for the harbor but for the ordinary people, when books and lectures make both seem distant."

Again, Kirk turned away. "You should ask your fiancée to meet you," he said, walking down the street. "I won't be there."

Their conversation quickly slipped from Kirk's mind, but he had too little else to think about that afternoon and it kept slipping back again. The words of a stranger on the street were probably not worth remembering, except that Travis was United States Navy, even if only a cadet.

In his teens, Kirk had applied to join the Naval Academy. His grades had been good, but not good enough.

Kirk shouldn't think of Travis, trying to understand the purpose of their conversation. Travis' engagement might not satisfy him; his fiancée might not save him from regret for losing Isla. Kirk knew everything he needed to know about Isla. He wanted to know more, but only because he wanted to know everything about her. They had time and time again for her to tell him.

On the other hand, Travis' engagement might satisfy him. His fiancée might, without regret.

Thinking about Travis seemed wrong. Kirk should be thinking

about Isla. He was thinking about Isla, but that only made him think about Travis and the mystery of which Kirk was being warned.

At the end of the shopping day, Isla closed the pottery store. There, as he was whenever she finished work on a weekend, stood Kirk.

"Let's eat somewhere special tonight," said Kirk, before he kissed. His kiss was brief, but he had something to say. "I have booked us a table at the Middleton Tavern."

"Can we afford it?"

"I can afford it," said Kirk. "I want to drink beer and eat crab cakes where I don't have to think about the world outside."

"I'll want to freshen up," said Isla.

"So will I," smiled Kirk.

The Middleton Tavern was near the harbor, a short walk from the pottery shop, but Isla left him to return to her home and he went to his. Kirk dressed for dinner, in much the same clothes he always wore and had worn that day, but they were neat and clean for the evening. Meeting Isla at her home, she'd dressed in something seductive, as all the clothes she wore away from work seduced him. Everything about her seduced him.

Kirk drove them back to the harbor, where he found a place to park from which they walked to the tavern. The tavern was also near the Kunta Kinte Memorial, but Kirk shouldn't think about that. He'd not mentioned Travis to Isla and wouldn't mention him, unless their conversation led him to do so.

Conversation between them might have been unusually stilted that evening; Kirk chastised himself for being distracted. The customers in the pottery store that day had been unremarkable, said Isla, because Kirk asked, unless an Australian wanting only Maryland-made pottery was remarkable.

In the tavern, they sat at a small table for two near a fireless fireplace, waiting for crab cakes. Kirk drank beer, Isla drank wine. (Isla had often observed that women drank wine while men drank alcoholic beer.)

"I would like to meet your Mom," said Kirk.

"That's a strange thing to say," said Isla. "She's in Denver, you know that."

"We could visit her. I've never seen Colorado."

Isla placed her hand on the table for him to hold. "We can

vacation there," she said, as he placed his hand on hers. "Colorado is beautiful." She then looked away. "My Mom," she said, shaking her head. "We can't see her. She's a junkie, no good to anyone."

"I'm sorry," said Kirk, wondering if that might have been her secret. "You have sisters…"

"Who spend their time feeding Mom so she doesn't starve herself to death," said Isla, facing him again. "Please, lover," she smiled, "I couldn't handle them again."

Kirk nodded. "I'm sorry," he said, but it seemed she deserved an explanation for his suggestion. "Today," said Kirk, "after you went into the pottery store, your ex-boyfriend Travis approached me."

Isla's eyes snapped wide open, her jaw fell, leaving her mouth gaping a little. "Is he still stalking me?" she asked, pulling her hand from his.

"He said he split from you."

"He lies," said Isla, shaking her head. "He lies, so I had to ask him to leave me alone. He wanted to marry me, but I can't marry a liar, so I asked him to go."

"I thought I should tell you," said Kirk.

"Don't believe anything he tells you," said Isla, "not about me." She took her glass of wine from the table and gulped down the rest of it. "I want to go home," she said. "I can't eat anything now."

A waiter brought two plates of crab cakes to the table. He set one before Isla and started to set one before Kirk.

"I want to go home," Isla again told Kirk. "Travis ruined my life and he's ruined this evening."

Kirk looked up at the waiter. "Can we please have them in a doggy bag?" asked Kirk.

"I hate that term," said Isla.

Kirk again looked at the waiter. "Can we please take them with us in a bag?" asked Kirk.

Their meals paid for by Kirk, carrying his crab cakes in a paper bag, Isla walked quickly from the tavern. Kirk followed her, the distance between them growing, except when she almost tripped on her heels.

Isla stopped at a street corner, looking around, until Kirk reached her. "The car is this way," he reminded her, leading her towards it.

They said nothing more as Kirk drove her home. Kirk didn't

play music as he often did in a silent car, so Isla felt reason to talk. She didn't.

"At three o'clock tomorrow afternoon," said Kirk, nearing her home, "Travis will be at the wharf."

She turned to face him. "Haven't you heard me?" she asked. "He's a stalker, he's a liar. Did he tell you he went to Denver? If he doesn't hurt you, he'll certainly hurt me."

Kirk concentrated upon driving. He parked his car near her home.

"You can keep all the crab cakes," said Isla, opening her door and stepping outside.

Kirk collected his bag of crab cakes from the rear passenger seat. He then stepped outside.

Isla saw the bag in his hand. "You eat them at your home," she told him.

Kirk placed the bag on the floor by the driving pedals, before closing the door and locking it. Hers was that kind of neighborhood.

At the front door to the building in which she lived, Isla faced him. "I don't want you seeing Travis," she told him.

"I won't," answered Kirk.

"Yes, you will. I don't want you to see him, but you will."

"I won't."

"I don't want you to believe him, but you will." She unlocked and opened the door to her building. "I can't see you for lunch tomorrow," she said, stepping inside.

Before Kirk could follow her, Isla closed the solid timber door. Alone, unable to see her, Kirk stood outside the building. He waited, giving her time to open the door. There was no reason to knock.

Finally, he left. Watching strangers without meeting their eyes, Kirk walked slowly back to his car.

Sunday lunchtime was strange without her. Shortly before three o'clock, Kirk arrived at the harbor. People rarely read plaques anymore but, for the first time waiting there, Kirk read the 1981 plaque on the Kunta Kinte memorial. It commemorated the arrival to Annapolis Harbor of the eighteenth-century African slave immortalized by Alex Haley in his twentieth-century novel *Roots*, along with all the others coming in bondage whose toil, character, and ceaseless struggle for freedom helped to make these United

States. Nearby, a bronze representation of Haley sat reading his bronze book to bronze boys and girls.

Again, a solitude in which Kirk stood was interrupted by the sound of Travis, standing beside him. "Experts believe Kunta Kinte didn't exist," said Travis.

Kirk turned towards him, again in uniform. He'd not come to hear anything more about Kunta Kinte.

"Haley invented him to tell a story," said Travis, "but we're too determined to believe his story to listen to experts, unless they say what we already believe."

"Isla exists," Kirk told him.

Travis smiled. "Or did someone invent her to tell a story?"

"She says she dropped you," replied Kirk, "because you invent things. She says I can't trust you."

"Don't trust me or her, not about everything. Consider the evidence for yourself."

"What evidence, Travis? What evidence do I have, but no evidence? What does that tell me?"

"Ask Isla about her mother's son," said Travis. "Ask her what happened to Irvin Peale?"

"She had a brother?" asked Kirk.

"Irvin Peale was the loneliest of loneliest boys, in a house without a father and a mother who hated both of them for it. Nobody hated his sisters, but they hated him, so he killed himself."

Kirk stepped backwards. "Poor Isla," he said, shaking his head. "We can't blame her for that. I should go to her now."

Leaving Travis and the harbor behind, Kirk strode away, along the streets and up the hill towards the Maryland State House, State Circle, and pottery shop. Inside the shop, Isla was talking to a customer. Kirk proceeded past the tables of pottery and around the counter, grabbed her, and kissed her.

If that kiss was long, even by the length of their kisses, then it still wasn't long enough. Eventually, if only to breathe, Kirk pulled away. He continued holding her arms.

Isla looked at the customer. Thus Kirk looked.

The customer, an elderly woman, smiled. "I won't detain you," she said, taking her purse from her handbag and several notes from her purse. "You keep the change." She laid some notes on the counter near Isla. "I don't need a receipt. I don't need wrapping." She took her small shining glazed pottery away with her.

Isla looked back at Kirk. Her eyes darted between his.

"Travis told me about Irvin," said Kirk. "I'll look after you, now."

She smiled, briefly. A tear caught the corner of her eye, before she dried it with her finger.

Kirk pulled her closer to him, so the side of her head rested against his face. "Don't be afraid."

She pulled away from him. "Can I see you after work?" she asked. "I can see you in the park over the road."

"Of course, lover," he smiled, before quickly kissing her again. She was at work, after all, with other customers in the store. Kirk hurried past the tables back to the door, careful not to knock any pottery to the floor.

Instead of walking that Sunday afternoon, Kirk killed time in the park across the road: the park of trees in which the Maryland State House rested. Aside from Kirk, the only people there on Sundays were probably tourists, and there were few of them.

Kirk walked around, examining a bell. He read a plaque. He sat on the grass and on the steps heading up from the sidewalk, never out of sight of the pottery store.

Streetlamps began shining, before they were needed. The few tourists became fewer, until only Kirk was there.

Soon after closing time, with the sun out of sight and afternoon becoming dark, Isla stepped out from the store. After glancing at Kirk watching her from the top of the stairs to the park, she closed and locked the shop door behind her. She hurried across the sidewalk, checked for traffic that wasn't there, and hurried across the road and sidewalk up the stairs to Kirk.

There, he kissed her again, his arms around her and hers around him. He spun her around him, kissing her, oblivious to everything else. Their kiss was long, to make up for the few kisses they'd had since Travis intruded upon them.

When Kirk tired, they stopped spinning. Kirk stepped back, facing her, he took her hands in his and stepped forward again, kissing her again. Travis had been an intrusion they needed, freeing them from a separation between them Kirk hadn't noticed, until it had gone.

Again, Kirk stepped back, their hands still holding each other's, facing each other. "Please, lover," he told her, "tell me everything. I'll love you and treasure you whatever your pains: whatever your story. I can't bring Irvin back to you, but I can be sky in which you smile to think of him and the pillow into which you cry missing him."

Isla pulled her hands from Kirk. She turned her eyes from him, starting to walk along the path through the park. "I don't smile to think of Irvin," she said, as Kirk followed close behind her. "I don't cry to miss him."

"You must miss him," said Kirk, almost beside her. "You must talk about your feelings."

Isla stopped and faced him. "Why must I talk about my feelings?" she asked him. "Why can't I talk to you about everything else in my life without mentioning Irvin? Why can't you love and protect me without you ever mentioning him again?"

Kirk stood facing her with only her and him in sight, on that public path in that darkening park. Near them was the most important public building in Maryland, but no law of the state or lawmaker knew he and Isla were there.

She faced him, staring at him. If she expected him to say something, then he didn't know what to say. If she expected him to kiss her again, then he couldn't. If she expected him to hold her, then he wouldn't.

"I killed Irvin," she told him, raising her voice, "all right, I killed him."

Kirk stepped back from her. "You killed your brother?"

"No!" she snapped, "I killed me."

Kirk stepped further back, off the path onto the grass unsure underfoot. "Killed you?" he gasped, shaking his head, trying to shut ideas out of his head as much as he was trying to hold them inside.

"I am Irvin Peale," she cried. "I wish I wasn't, and I'm not. I'm Isla: the woman you love. Why can't I be Isla?"

Kirk stepped further back, almost slipping on the grass but correcting himself. She started towards him, her arms open to him, but he stepped further back. If she wasn't a crazy woman, she was a crazy man. He turned and ran away, across the grass to rejoin the path away from her. He reached the steps and, with a hand on the railing, leapt over several steps and then several more, before almost stumbling onto the sidewalk.

Without checking for traffic, Kirk ran over State Circle and down Francis Street. Streets and corners once familiar became confused, but he ran downhill and along busy Main Street until he was again at the harbor among people, where a little more daylight remained.

By the harbor was the wharf. To the statues of the storyteller and children but not to them ran Kirk. When he reached them, pressing his hand on the memorial block so he didn't fall over, almost stumbling into Alex Haley, Kirk looked around for Travis.

Ahead of him by the water was a naval cadet in uniform, walking away from him so Kirk could only see him from behind. By his side was a woman, holding his hand as he held hers.

"Travis!" called Kirk, running towards them. "Travis."

The cadet didn't respond. He and the woman continued walking by the harbor towards the river, away from the town.

Kirk reached him and put his hand on his shoulder. "Travis," he said panting, as the cadet faced him.

The cadet wasn't Travis. He looked at the woman.

"I'm sorry," said Kirk, stepping away. "You looked like someone I know."

The cadet and his girl turned away from Kirk. They resumed walking.

Kirk stood alone, moving around, still panting but slowly recovering his breath. People strolling Annapolis of a late afternoon and early evening strolled by the harbor, where the river waters lapped boats rarely leaving their berths. Dozens of men, women, and children strolled, some looking out to the waters and some to each other. None of them could Kirk ask about Isla Peale, about Irvin Peale, about the death of either or deaths of both of them.

His and Isla's past intimacy haunted him. Kirk grimaced, but that did not change anything. His arms and legs had become clammy in his clothes because she'd touched them; he shouldn't think of Irvin being she.

Near the wharf was the Middleton Tavern. Kirk ran back there, rushed inside, and took a glass of cold water.

He swilled the water around his mouth, looked around, and ran outside. At a patch of ground away from people, he spat the dirty water out. He swilled more water from the glass and spat that out, until the mouth that kissed Irvin couldn't dirty the water anymore.

Kirk wanted to be sick, to cleanse his insides, but couldn't, not there. He returned the glass to the tavern and returned to the open air, becoming night.

He stumbled back to the Kunta Kinte memorial, if only for the chance Travis might be there. Kirk didn't know what more Travis could tell him or he could tell Travis, but he wanted to ask and he wanted to talk.

The inscription on another plaque spoke of strong family connections and pride in a person's heritage, founding the strength of the human spirit. Kirk laughed.

Isla's voice interrupted him. "I thought I'd find you here," she said – he said – standing near Kirk, "looking for Travis and a meeting of the Hating Isla Peale Club."

Kirk stepped back from him. "You're a man," Kirk told him.

"I'm Isla."

"Taking a woman's name doesn't make you a woman."

Isla held out his thin arms, wrists, and hands, leaving behind his long curved figure. "Don't you see a woman when you look at me?" asked Isla. His voice was soft, like a woman's voice, without obvious effort on his part.

From his delicate face to his smallish feet and everything in between, Isla appeared every bit a woman; he always had, through Kirk's time knowing him. His cheek bones were high, jaw soft, and neck thin. No Adam's apple protruded from his throat. His shoulders were rounded, at a time many women wore shoulder pads wanting to appear a little masculine. His waist was narrow, hips rounded, and everything else the hourglass that women wanted to be and men wanted women to be, but none of it meant anything in a man.

This was not a woman to hold. It was a man from whom to step away. As for Isla's mind, Kirk never knew it.

"I want to be me," pleaded Isla.

"This isn't you, Isla, or Irvin; your name doesn't matter. A terrific surgeon, or many surgeons, made you look like a woman but can't make you a woman. Surgery can't change your gender. It can only conceal the gender you've got."

Isla dropped his arms to his side. There was nothing beautiful about him. There never was.

"I want a woman," resumed Kirk. "I want a family…"

"We can be a family…"

"No, we can't. All your surgery can't make us a family. Being parents takes something that you and I can't be together."

"We could employ a child bearer?" said Isla.

"I'm not employing motherhood. I need a woman and you need a woman, you don't need to be a woman, if it's not too late for you now."

"Don't your care about me?"

"I care about you more than you care about yourself. You're lying so much to yourself I can't worry about you lying to me every moment I've known you. I should pity you, but you don't pity yourself. I want you to get well, Irvin. I want you to be content being a man, without the agonies that make you wish so much that you weren't. I can't help you if you won't help yourself. I'm not sure I can help you even then, but don't expect me to tell you that you're something you're not. If you want to live life in a lie, then I can't stop you, but I don't have to join you in lying."

"But you did love me," begged Isla, "didn't you?"

"I will never love a man like I can love a woman. I will never love you like I can love a woman. The feelings I had for you were my ignorance, but I'm not ignorant now and I won't become ignorant again. We're finished as a couple, Isla, and yes, it's because you're a man. Whatever that makes you think of me, I don't care, but it's not going to change. I can't get back the time I spent with you, but I don't have to waste time with you now I can spend with a woman."

Isla looked down at the ground. He could seem so frail, thought Kirk: a weak, self-deprecating man in a nice woman's dress.

"Whether you should undergo more surgery to correct your last blunders," said Kirk, "I don't know, but you can at least stop injecting chemicals and hormones that shouldn't be in you. You can let your body be what it wants to be, instead of punishing it for not being what you want it to be, because you hate your life so painfully much."

Kirk gave Isla time to answer. Instead, Isla continued looking at the ground. The night was building around them, but for a streetlamp close to Kirk.

"Goodbye, Isla," said Kirk. "I wish you a mountain of happiness, but you're not going to get that living a lie. If you ever want to be yourself, Irvin, then maybe we can be friends; we'd have to see then. We can eat crab cakes and drink at the Middleton Tavern; I don't care whether you drink beer, wine, or water. We can talk about women we go out with, those we want to go out with, and those we have been out with, but never a woman you're pretending to be."

9 MY FATHER'S PLACE

Along the Jersey Shore, the smell of salt air could be so normal that residents stopped sensing it. That was, unless they'd been away, inside for a time, or a rush of wind beyond the normal breeze made the salt pervasive.

Among the places to be inside were the bars and restaurants. Along East Ocean Avenue, Sea Bright, Thomasina Vecoli managed an eatery and pub, with a dining room, known as My Father's Place because it was: her elderly father had enjoyed it enough to invest all his savings to buy it. (Calling it a pub fitted with his sociable sense of the place.) He ate there, drank there, occasionally played pool with patrons on the pool table there, although not very well, and most of all conversed with customers, while Thomasina worked.

The business employed twenty-five people, none of whom were anything like the young woman who slouched in her chair across the table from Thomasina that Monday morning, two decades into the twenty-first century. Lying on the table in front of Thomasina was her printed copy of the young woman's job application.

At least, Thomasina guessed she was a woman. Her name Sigma hadn't given anything away.

Sigma's clothes were black, as were the tee shirts, slacks, and trousers that waitresses and waiters often wore, but hers were baggy, falling around her. They made her look a little plump, as she might have been. They made her white skin ghostly, as uniforms didn't make working people.

Adding to her ghostliness was her black hair. It was too black on an American to be anything but dyed.

Her ears weren't pierced, as they were among most of the waitresses. Instead, a side of her nose and skin above her mouth were pierced.

Such of Sigma's shoulders as were visible were feminine shoulders; more than anything else, they convinced Thomasina that Sigma was a woman. On her left shoulder, reaching onto her neck, were tattoos of Chinese characters, along with a tattooed dragon.

High on her right arm, partially covered by portions of her black blouse, or dress, or shirt, or whatever she wore, was a tattoo Thomasina could not decipher. It might have been a horse, or a thunderstorm, or a very bad dream. It might have been anything.

On Sigma's fingernails was black nail polish. It seemed relatively innocuous, more noticeable on other women.

Along her fingers were several thick silver rings, much like the several silver bangles, of varying thicknesses and diameters, around her wrists. They made Thomasina's single gold wedding ring on her ring finger modest by comparison. They also made Thomasina's ring never more elegant.

Sigma wasn't the first person Thomasina had seen to dress as she did. Nor was she the first such person to apply for a job at My Father's Place. If Thomasina and her father offered her a job, then she would be the first such person to get one.

"Have you a family name?" Thomasina asked her.

"I don't believe in families," answered Sigma.

When she opened her mouth to speak, Thomasina thought she saw a piercing in the young woman's tongue. Thomasina paused from listening to her words to study her mouth. Yes, her tongue was pierced.

"Families inhibit personal freedom," finished Sigma.

Thomasina glanced towards her father, sitting at another table, reading a newspaper there as he'd done every morning since before buying the business. On the table with him, as it always was, lay his tweed cap; he only wore it outside. "My father," Thomasina told Sigma, motioning towards him, "he's over there."

Sigma didn't look. "If that's your thing," she said. "You haven't asked me what pronoun I want you to use to describe me."

Thomasina had heard of people expecting to be asked that question, and of universities and other bodies instructing everyone to ask it. She'd never before heard anyone expect her to ask it.

"Are you going to ask?" persisted Sigma, with more presumption than Thomasina ever volunteered in her younger days of being interviewed for jobs.

"Aren't you female?" asked Thomasina.

Sigma sighed. She shook her head and looked around, as if hoping for someone to tell her what fool she'd encountered, before looking back at Thomasina. "You should have asked," she said.

"But you are female?"

"You should ask me what gender I am and what pronoun you should use to describe me," Sigma lectured her, "without presuming my answer."

Thomasina sat staring at her. Sigma stared back at her. Their time together was no longer a job interview, even if Sigma didn't know it. Thomasina wasn't giving her a waitressing job or any other job, but with a little free time that morning, she would enjoy the experience. "What gender are you, Sigma?"

"Today," she answered, before pulling an electronic device from a pocket Thomasina hadn't previously noticed and checking the display, "at ten forty-three this morning, I am female."

Thomasina continued staring at her. Sigma returned her electronic device to the pocket that Thomasina couldn't see anymore.

Again, Sigma stared at Thomasina. "And?" asked Sigma.

"And?" asked Thomasina.

"You should ask me what pronouns to use to describe me."

"Aren't you still female?" asked Thomasina, before checking the clock on the wall, "at ten forty-four this morning?"

"I'll tell you if I've changed genders, now that you've asked, because I'm trying to be helpful, but you don't know what pronouns I want you to use to describe me."

"Aren't females 'she' and 'her'?" asked Thomasina.

Sigma scoffed. "You're compartmentalizing me, putting me in a group I might not want to join."

Thomasina again stared at her; she was probably right, about that. "What pronoun should I use to refer to you?" asked Thomasina.

"Pronouns," Sigma corrected her, stressing the plural form. "There are personal pronouns, possessive pronouns…" Sigma hadn't seemed to be a person concerned with grammar, although she clearly struggled to continue reciting her list, before finishing, "…and more."

"All right then," nodded Thomasina. "I'll play. What pronouns should I use to refer to you?"

"'She' and 'her'," replied Sigma, "but that's my choice, not yours to impose upon me. Would you want me to presume your gender and the pronouns I should use to describe you?"

"Go ahead and presume," said Thomasina, with her full-bodied brown hair, closely hugging dress that never meant to hide (or amplify) her ample bust and hips, along with a face she hoped was decidedly feminine. "I hope my gender is unmistakable."

"Are you transgender or cisgender?"

"Do I look transgender?" asked Thomasina, more surprised than ever in that surprising conversation.

"I never can tell."

"Isn't cisgender just being normal?"

"What is your gender?" asked Sigma. "What pronoun should I use to describe you?"

"I'm temperamental bean curd," answered Thomasina. "You should refer to me as 'Noo' and 'Vark'."

Sigma had listened without moving, so obviously concentrating upon Thomasina's answer that Thomasina wondered if she really was. "I should make note of that," said Sigma, reaching for her invisible pocket and removing her electronic device again.

"Oops," said Thomasina, jumping a little in her chair. "I'm female now," she explained, much cheekier than she normally was. "You can refer to me as 'she' or 'her'." The other pronouns, Sigma could realize for herself.

Without recording anything, so far as Thomasina noticed, Sigma calmly returned her electronic device to her hidden pocket. She must have felt she could remember Thomasina's gender and those pronouns without needing to note them. Thomasina was rather pleased about that.

Sigma removed a packet of cigarettes from a pocket of whatever it was she wore; a blouse, perhaps. She also removed a small lighter.

"You can't smoke in here," Thomasina told her. "This is a public bar."

"Who's going to tell?"

"I'm going to tell," said Thomasina. "Did you buy those? You're not twenty-one."

"My boyfriend buys them out of state."

"We can't have people working here breaking the law. We could be shut down."

"I can't start the job today," insisted Sigma, putting her packet of cigarettes and lighter back in her pocket. "I'm meditating on the beach at noon, and I don't know when my consciousness will return."

"What makes you think I'm giving you the job?"

Sigma laughed. "When I woke this morning," she said, "I knew I'd get it. I felt it. You need me."

There really wasn't any point, or fun, in contradicting her. Instead, Thomasina checked the printed copy of Sigma's job application, lying on the table. "You give your age as eighteen," she said.

The pub served alcohol, as public bars did. American law required people to be twenty-one years of age to buy alcohol, although New Jersey law generally allowed those at least eighteen years of age to serve it. They could change gender at any age.

"Are they eighteen Earth years," asked Thomasina, "or do you simply identify as eighteen?"

Sigma smiled, nodding. "I see what you're doing," she said. "That's good." Thomasina also smiled. "I identify with Earth years."

Thomasina stopped smiling. She looked again at Sigma's job application.

"You might want to make a note of that," said Sigma.

Thomasina didn't. "I think I'll remember," she said, as she read. "Is stupid a gender?" asked Thomasina, without looking up.

Sigma didn't reply. They'd long moved so far from being a job interview, Thomasina was simply sitting with a person in the pub. Sigma wasn't a customer, as were the people with whom her father conversed, but she sat where customers sat. Thomasina didn't expect Sigma to buy anything that day or any other day. When Sigma eventually realized she wasn't getting the job, Thomasina expected her to leave and never return. People like Sigma ate and drank in My Father's Place, but not after they'd failed to get jobs there.

"I see you went to school in Reno," said Thomasina, finally looking back at Sigma.

"My boyfriend and I needed space, not from each other, but from everyone else."

"If your boyfriend stops identifying as a boy," asked Thomasina, "does he stop being your boyfriend?"

"I call him my boyfriend because that's how he told me to refer to him," Sigma explained. "He doesn't like pronouns. He thinks they deny him his freedom."

"You both do like your freedoms, don't you," remarked Thomasina, "but aren't you referring to him by pronouns now?"

Sigma smiled. "I am, aren't I?" she said. "That's my thing, and as long as he never finds out, I'm being respectful."

Thomasina carefully considered Sigma's words, somewhat surprised that anything Sigma said required careful consideration. Maybe, in the context of everything else about Sigma, her words were relatively reasonable, but only relative to everything else she'd said. "I'm free," said Thomasina, "even when I hear people refer to me by pronouns."

"You talk to my boyfriend about it," said Sigma, "although I guess you'll never meet him. He can't know that I work here. He doesn't understand polyamory and might mess everything up."

With every new turn in their conversation, Sigma took them somewhere stranger. "I don't understand polyamory," said Thomasina.

"Where have you been?"

"Working," answered Thomasina, "but I suppose I should be glad you have a boyfriend."

Sigma turned her head to the side, before smiling. "What I desire today might not be what I desire tomorrow," she said. "Our endless choice of genders must mean we have an endless choice of sexualities."

Again, their conversation had turned. Again, Thomasina thought. From the perspective in which Sigma stood, from the presumption on which her conclusion was predicated, she was probably correct; nonsense led logically to more nonsense. "Did you hear that from someone?" asked Thomasina.

"How did you know?" asked Sigma. "All love is equal, we say."

"You might," said Thomasina, before being facetious. "Is your love at least limited to adults?"

Sigma smiled. "Whatever their age," she said, "people have the right to consent." (Thomasina's sense of humor couldn't match Sigma's sense of liberty.) "People consent to desires innate to them."

She must have heard a lot, thought Thomasina, if only from one person. "Is your love at least limited to human beings?" inquired Thomasina.

Sigma laughed. "Aren't you the prude?"

Thomasina grappled for imagination. "Are your desires at least confined to organic matter?" she asked.

Again Sigma laughed, louder this time. "Aren't you boring?" she said. "Don't box me in with your prejudices. Don't hold me to your rules."

No longer could Thomasina try to be facetious with Sigma, she wasn't smart enough to stay ahead of whoever Sigma quoted. "Have you any restrictions at all upon whom or what you'll love?" asked Thomasina.

Sigma sat up a little. "I have my standards," she insisted. "I don't love you."

From other people, Thomasina might have taken umbrage. From Sigma, her words were probably just as well. "I don't love you," replied Thomasina.

Sigma laughed, moving Thomasina to laugh with her, as friends might laugh together. "I'm thinking that your thing isn't loving people anyway," smiled Sigma. "Not loving me is to be expected, when you only love one person, maybe none."

She could be too complicated for Thomasina to understand. There wasn't any reason to try. "When you do get a job," asked Thomasina, in their spirit of conversation, hoping that Sigma didn't presume she referred to a job in Thomasina's father's place, "where will you tell your boyfriend, if that's what he then is, you go each day and night?"

"Out," answered Sigma. "He goes out and that's all I know. I go out and that's all he knows."

"So you don't know if he has a job?" asked Thomasina. "He might be a stockbroker, or a cardiovascular surgeon?"

"He is very smart," nodded Sigma. "He plays video games."

Thomasina sat quietly. Not everything Sigma said commanded Thomasina to think about it.

A waitress in her black tee-shirt and slacks walked past them, collecting Sigma's attention. Sigma watched her walk away, before looking back at Thomasina. "I shouldn't have to wear the uniform," said Sigma.

"You wear black, anyway," Thomasina pointed out.

"This isn't black," insisted Sigma, placing her hands on the clothes covering her chest, looking over them as if looking over them proved something. "It's midnight."

"Midnight must get very black where you are."

"I'm an individual," insisted Sigma.

"Individuals can wear uniforms," replied Thomasina, "or does your individuality depend upon your clothes?"

"My clothes express me."

"Really?" checked Thomasina, but Sigma had made retorts too easy. "Mine don't."

"Don't they?"

"You're not the only person to dress as you dress."

"I'm the only person dressing as I dress in this place now," said Sigma.

Thomasina looked around. No more than ten customers were there, still well before lunchtime of a Monday, spread around the pub. Some sat in groups of two or three. A couple sat alone, as did Thomasina's father reading his newspaper at a table; if he had looked up from time to time to see if anybody invited conversation, he must have decided none did. None of the people dressed like Sigma, in any way.

"Your uniform would cover my tatts," complained Sigma.

"I hope so," said Thomasina. "My father would never employ a person with tattoos, although I convinced him we could employ people whose tattoos were hidden."

"My tatts are me," said Sigma. "They're unique. They identify me."

"Didn't you choose them from a catalogue?" guessed Thomasina.

"This combination is unique," insisted Sigma, "to me."

"How do you know?" asked Thomasina. "Have you checked, or do you simply identify as having a unique combination of common catalogue tattoos?"

"I think you're being silly," insisted Sigma. "I'm not sure I want to work here, with you."

Taking her printed copy of Sigma's job application in her hand, Thomasina stood up from her chair. "I introduce every job applicant to my father," said Thomasina, "if only for his amusement."

The introductions with her father were normally quick chats and smiles, which ensured that applicants understood the importance of Thomasina's father to the place. If Thomasina indicated to her father that she wanted to hire a person and he indicated to her that he preferred she didn't, then she wouldn't. He never had. Of course, she'd never indicated to him she wanted to hire a person like Sigma, although he'd spoken with customers like her. He'd spoken to every kind of customer, at one time or another.

"He would like to meet you," Thomasina told Sigma, more than simply because he liked to meet interviewees. "He's nicer than I am."

"This won't take long, will it?" asked Sigma, standing up from her chair. "I have the beach to get to."

"The beach has been there for thousands of years," said Thomasina. "It will still be there when we're finished."

"I know," insisted Sigma, "silly."

Thomasina led Sigma to Thomasina's father at his table. "Papa," she said to him.

He looked up from his newspaper to Thomasina and Sigma standing there. He folded his newspaper closed, as he always closed newspapers and magazines to talk with people.

At the table were three other chairs. Thomasina sat in one. "This is Sigma," she told him. "Sigma has applied for a waitressing job here. I am as interested in offering her a job as I was interested in offering one to that girl from Honolulu." Thomasina hadn't offered a job to the girl from Honolulu.

Sigma continued to stand. She looked down at Thomasina's father.

"Would you like to sit, Sigma?" he asked her. "I'm Mister D'Amato." Thomasina's father offered what he still called his Christian name to customers with whom he chatted. He didn't offer it to employees, not initially. "You can call me Salvatore."

"I'm in a hurry," Sigma told him.

Thomasina continued introducing Sigma to her father. "Sigma moved to the Shore from Reno," she told him.

"This is as far as I can get from Reno," said Sigma, looking around the pub, "without getting too hot, too cold, or winding up in another casino town."

"I don't gamble," said Salvatore. Neither did Thomasina.

"The only beaches near Reno are on lakes," Sigma told him, "or selling fro-yo."

"That's frozen yoghurt," Thomasina explained to her father, without understanding Sigma's reference.

"Lakeside beaches can be nice," smiled Salvatore, "but I do like salty air."

Sigma perked up. "Come with us," she said to him, before turning to Thomasina. "Come with me to the beach!"

"I'm working," said Thomasina. "I can't just leave."

"You can," insisted Sigma, turning around. "I can. We all can." She ran from the table to the door, her arms dragging behind her as she did. She pulled open the door and departed.

Thomasina looked at her father. "I could leave her there," she told him, "but I've not told her that she's not getting the job."

She rose from her chair, walked to the door and stepped outside. Unable to see Sigma, Thomasina proceeded to the nearby street corner.

At the far end of the short and quiet street, Sigma stood waving her black-cloaked arms and hands, facing back at Thomasina. "Here!" Sigma called out, summoning Thomasina. "Here!" Behind her was the six-foot tall ocean levee of roughly dumped rocks, holding back the beach beyond it.

"Wait," said Thomasina walking towards her. The breeze was all the more salty with every step towards the Atlantic Ocean, without being as loud as it had been other days.

Sigma looked around her. Even if she climbed the rocks and sand to the top of the levee, amidst the open ocean air, a fence there would keep her from the beach.

Thomasina knew Sigma would need to continue along the street to find a staircase over the levee. Sigma appeared not to know.

Sigma again removed her packet of cigarettes and lighter from her pockets. Deftly, her fingers pushed and wrist flicked a cigarette up from the packet. She offered it to Thomasina.

"I don't smoke," said Thomasina, as she reached her.

"We should drink," said Sigma, lighting her cigarette.

With the breeze from the sea, Thomasina stepped back and around her, upwind. Sigma's cigarette smoke never reached her.

"Can you get us a bottle of Bourbon?" asked Sigma.

The presumption of her question didn't need Thomasina's response, any more than did Thomasina's distaste for whiskey. "I'm not drinking alcohol at present," said Thomasina, before resting her hand on her belly. She felt only the slightest bump, to someone already knowing what it was. "My husband and I…"

"Don't you find marriage restrictive?" asked Sigma, puffing her cigarette.

Thomasina smiled. "We're expecting a baby boy," she said.

"You don't know it's a boy."

Sigma seemed more interested in the unborn child's gender

than in Thomasina carrying the child. "There are lots of things I don't know," smiled Thomasina, "but I know this is a boy. The ultrasound revealed it."

"You don't know," insisted Sigma. "You don't know your child's gender until it is old enough to discover that gender for itself and tell you."

"Why do you call him an 'it,' may I ask?"

"I'm trying not to categorize it. I'm trying to let it be free."

"You're categorizing him as an 'it,'" retorted Thomasina, enjoying herself. "What will you do when he's old enough to tell you that he's not an it: that he has a gender and he's masculine?"

"That's awful," said Sigma, smoking away. "Your child might need you until we've found a way to free children from parents, but do you think your child will like you? Do you think your child will love you?"

Thomasina laughed. "I know better than to think children love their parents these days," she said. "Do you like or love your mother and father?"

"I don't have a father," answered Sigma, pausing for long puffs of her cigarette. "I never had a father."

"You must have had a father."

"I had two mothers."

"You had a mother and a father. Your father might have never met you, he might be no more than a genetic contribution, but he's still your father. Only one woman contributed to your genes; you only have one mother."

Sigma took a particularly long mouthful of smoke. She slowly exhaled. "You're dumb," she said.

"I might be, but not about this."

"How would you feel if that child of yours grew into someone like my mothers, who didn't want a stale, old-fashioned marriage like yours?"

"I'd be hurt," admitted Thomasina, because she thought Sigma should hear it. "I'd be devastated. I know that I shouldn't, because there are more forces affecting children's upbringings than simply their parents, but I'd feel that I failed as a parent. If I fail as a parent, then I fail as a person."

Whatever response Thomasina hoped to elicit from Sigma, she didn't get. "Some people," said Sigma, pointedly including Thomasina among them, "shouldn't be allowed to be parents."

"Sigma!" snapped Thomasina, stepping a little further back. The novelty of the morning had gone. Thomasina had nothing more to experience from her. "I interviewed another girl earlier this morning," she told Sigma. "I think I'll offer her the job."

"Why give her the job?"

"I think she'd fit in better than you would."

"I could fit in," Sigma insisted, "if you'll fit in with me. These things have to be done both ways. I fitted in when I was in Reno, until I didn't want to fit in anymore."

"I don't think I'd fit in at Reno," quipped Thomasina. "You wouldn't fit in here not just with me, but with another twenty-five staff I have to consider, as well as our customers."

"That's discriminatory!" complained Sigma.

"Why is it discriminatory?"

"You're not employing me because you don't think I'd fit in."

"How else am I supposed to choose between applicants, if not by how well you'd fit in?"

"You could employ both of us?"

"I can't afford to employ both of you."

The ash from Sigma's cigarette had become long and fell to the ground; she had forgotten to smoke. "You could fire one of the employees you've already got," said Sigma. "Do you employ too many men?"

Thomasina didn't immediately know the proportion of her employees who were men, although she knew each of them well enough to calculate the proportion in her head, if she wanted to. She only knew that her employees were all men or women and that she'd never needed to ask which. "What if I fired a man to employ you, but then you identified as a man?"

"I could promise not to identify as a man."

"What about your personal freedom?" asked Thomasina, enjoying herself again. The more she thought about Sigma, the less she cared about anything Sigma said. "Do you want to miss out on a gender one day because of your job?"

"You should think about that," said Sigma, "before you're so hostile."

"You could identify as having the job," smiled Thomasina. "You could identify as a waitress working here."

"Or I could be a waiter working here," said Sigma, "or a wait-thing, a wait-person. I'd have to see at the time."

Thomasina nodded. She had no reason not to nod to anything Sigma said, she thought.

Sigma took another long mouthful of smoke and tar from her cigarette. "I've got the job!" she cried out. "I'm employed!"

"I don't identify as your employer," Thomasina corrected her. "I identify as a person who didn't give you a job."

Sigma fell silent. She seemed to think carefully about her situation, as she'd not obviously thought about much since Thomasina met her that morning, if ever. "What about my rights?" asked Sigma.

"What about mine?"

Sigma shook her head, her face reddening. "I won't drink in your pub," she told Thomasina, throwing her cigarette to the ground. "I wouldn't eat from your eatery if you begged me."

"You don't drink or eat there now. I've never seen you."

"I saw the people when I went in. Nobody smoked."

"Nobody smokes in bars and restaurants in New Jersey."

"None of them looked like me; they made me feel like I wasn't meant to be there."

In truth, thought Thomasina, they probably never noticed her. They wouldn't have cared where she was.

"Why would I eat there?" asked Sigma. "Why would I drink there?"

"If my staff looked like you," said Thomasina, "customers wouldn't come."

"Other customers would come. I'd come."

"How many people are like you?"

"My friend Peach is like me."

"Do all your friends have names like Sigma and Peach?"

"Peach couldn't get a job at the Ocean Place Resort, but she met a nice person outside who didn't care about her tatts and rings."

"Have you thought about dressing for job interviews in clothes that fit you, covering your tattoos?" asked Thomasina. "Have you considered removing your piercings for work and brushing your hair?"

"That's what I am."

"Really?" asked Thomasina. "My clothes and appearance aren't what I am, but they keep my father in business and let me earn an income."

Sigma looked up and down over Thomasina's dress and shoes. "Is that what you normally wear?" mocked Sigma. "Why can't you take me as I am?"

"You're not presenting yourself as you are," Thomasina lectured her. "You're a caricature: one that people might like to gawk at from a distance in Reno, but not one they want serving them food and drink in Sea Bright."

Sigma's legs moved a small way apart, in a gesture of confrontation more obvious to Thomasina than it might have been to Sigma. "I'm going to find my friends and we're going to come back here at ten o'clock tomorrow," she told her. "We'll see how mean you are when I'm not on my own."

"Is this how you think you'll get a job," asked Thomasina, "in New Jersey?"

"That's up to you, isn't it?"

Sigma turned and ran along the street between the levee and the pub, away from Thomasina. A little overweight to run, Sigma ran clumsily, towards the stairs by which she could traverse the levee and reach the beach, if that was where she was going.

Sigma's burning cigarette and ash lay on the street. Thomasina stood over each of them in turn, pressing a sole of her shoes onto them, crushing and extinguishing them.

Slowly, a little more tired than a mere job interview should have left her, Thomasina ambled back to the pub, leaving the ocean air behind her. Inside, her father sat waiting at the table, watching her return. He'd not resumed reading his newspaper. He'd not started a conversation with anyone else.

Thomasina picked up her printed copy of Sigma's job application. She screwed it into a ball and dropped it into the wastebasket behind the bar.

Shortly before ten o'clock the next morning, instead of sitting at a table with a newspaper, Salvatore stood at the open pub entrance, the only doors at the front of the building. The weather was mild that morning. The wind was down. On his head was his tweed cap; he might have been the only man in Sea Bright to wear one. Thomasina stood beside him.

A customer came. "Salvatore," he said, "Thomasina." He went inside. Staff inside would tend to him.

Across the wide avenue, beyond the parking area, a figure stood. Of about Sigma's height and build, in so far as those lazy black clothes suggested, it could have been her. The figure certainly seemed dressed as she'd dressed the previous day.

Another figure joined her. That might have been Sigma, as might the next and the next to join her, although that one's hair might have been paler. It could be hard to tell from a distance. By ten o'clock, there must have been fifteen of them standing there.

When no more came, they started walking towards Salvatore, Thomasina, and their pub. They walked in an unkempt armada, waiting for pauses in the traffic, until they entered the car park. At the head of the horde came Sigma. She stopped ten or so yards short of Thomasina and Salvatore.

The people behind her came to each side of her. They slowly formed a line a person deep, standing with their feet small spaces apart much as Sigma had stood one day earlier, those fifteen wayward warriors, of sorts.

They might have been men or women, old or young; Thomasina couldn't tell. Dyes and powders as much as clothes and jewelry concealed the human beings within them. Thomasina wondered whether they really knew.

For people presumably all so boastful of their individuality, those fifteen in a row could be uncommonly conforming. All of their clothes, however hard those clothes were to particularize, were dark; most of those clothes were black, or midnight. Their sameness made them uniforms, for people who all presumably refused to wear uniforms.

Their hairstyles of many colors and stabbings from their scalps must have made them feel unique among normal people. Standing with each other in that line in their intensity, those hairstyles only made them all look the same. They'd become indistinguishable not from the world, but from each other. That was probably the idea.

From the center of the line, Sigma stepped forward. The garb she wore might have been the same she'd worn the previous day. It might not; all her clothes might have looked like that.

"Are you scared now?" she called to Thomasina, with deepness to her voice drawn from the throng around her.

Salvatore stepped forward, away from his daughter, towards Sigma and her horde. Sigma and her horde stepped back.

He again stepped forward. They again stepped back.

"Boo!" snapped Salvatore.

A person beside Sigma turned and ran away. So did the next

person, then another, and another, as fast as each of them could but not very fast, under all of their clothes and other baggage. When Sigma was the last person left, she also turned and ran. They each ran away from Salvatore in the direction that took him, her, or something else away from him as quickly as possible: fanning out in straight lines around people and cars with him standing at their center.

"Boo," he said again, not as loudly as the first time. They might have run faster.

10 SERVICE

"Ma'am?" cried out a voice from the public side of the bar. "I'm Sir!"

Hearing the voice from her managerial office (its door was normally open) was Thomasina Vecoli, in her long orange maternity dress and with a baby bump beginning to show. The day was Tuesday, shortly before midday, when My Father's Place pub and eatery in Sea Bright, New Jersey was beginning to become busy for lunch. The cry could have been a man's or a woman's cry; cries loud enough could be hard to distinguish, especially when a woman was trying to sound like a man. Thomasina came out of her office to investigate.

"I'm sorry, Sir," the bartender answered the voice. "I thought you were a lady."

"Do I look like a lady?"

Thomasina walked around the counter and into the public bar area towards the person speaking. Two weeks earlier, Thomasina would have called the person's shirt and trousers black. They were something very, very dark.

Aged probably in the twenties and wearing men's platform black leather shoes, the person remained nevertheless short and a little overweight: much shorter than Thomasina and decidedly more overweight. The person's dark hair was cut short, as men's hair normally was, but the cheek and jaw bones were slight, clearly feminine. Held up in fury, the person's hands carried no jewelry beyond a thick men's sports watch on the left wrist. There was no nail polish on the fingers, but those fingers and hands were stubby and small. Most telling of all, in spite of the bagginess of the person's shirt, there were clearly women's breasts behind it.

"I am the manageress," said Thomasina. The person turned towards her. "I am sorry if there has been a misunderstanding…"

"Misunderstanding?" cried the person. "How would you feel if I called you a man?"

Thomasina smiled. "I might think of dressing more femininely," she said, although she could hardly be more feminine than wearing a maternity dress. No one had ever confused her for a man.

No clothes could make the person confronting her from a low height appear like a man. "I am obviously a man," the person nevertheless insisted; what might have been obvious to that person wasn't obvious to Thomasina. "Your barman is too dumb to see it."

The person spun back to face the bartender. He had started to serve another customer.

"I want a glass of beer," demanded the person, "cold beer."

Pausing from what he was doing, the bartender looked back at the person. He then looked at Thomasina.

Thomasina remained calm, summoning a barmaid to serve that other customer before again facing the person complaining. "I am sure that you're over twenty-one," said Thomasina, "but you understand that we must check people's identification to ensure they are."

"If you're sure, then why must you check?"

"It is the law," explained Thomasina.

"It's a stupid law."

"Some laws are stupid," said Thomasina, although she and the person clearly considered different laws stupid.

From a trouser pocket, the person removed a man's black wallet, opened it, and pulled from it a small plastic card. The person handed the card to Thomasina.

Less interested in the person's age than the person's name and gender, in so far as it was displayed on an Arizonan driver's license, Thomasina examined it. "Atlas Whalan," she read aloud, before calculating the small arithmetic in her head, "born, twenty-two years ago."

The license recorded Atlas' gender as male. Apparently issued a year earlier, the license might have been reissued because Atlas had changed name, gender, or both, in the eyes of the Arizona authorities, but those weren't Thomasina's eyes. Nothing could change Atlas' biology, not even changing her (not his, thought Thomasina) anatomy, if she'd done so or planned to do so. Thomasina knew not to say so aloud, not to Atlas.

"You're from Phoenix," said Thomasina, trying to be conversational. "The Jersey Shore is a long way from Phoenix."

"I move around a lot. I'm a gypsy."

"Does that mean you identify as a gypsy," asked Thomasina, "so you are a gypsy?"

Atlas stared at her; she might have been thinking. The bartender continued watching both of them, as did the barmaid and the customer she'd finished serving.

Thomasina returned the license to Atlas. "I've never met anyone named for a Titan god," said Thomasina. "Jesus, Mohammed, yes, but not a Titan god. Did your parents give you the name?"

Not that Thomasina could imagine any parent calling a child Atlas; that certainly wasn't a name she and her husband considered for their son. Even less would they have considered it for a daughter. No, two decades into twenty-first century America, Atlas was strictly a stage name, especially for women thinking they're men. No person could be further from the Titan god who held the sky aloft than the short squat figure of a woman standing pluckily before Thomasina.

"Give me a beer," demanded Atlas, "which you can give me for free for the bartender wrongly gendering me."

"Gendering?" asked Thomasina, slowly realizing what that new word must mean.

"If your barman is too dumb to know a person's gender," said Atlas, "he should have asked."

A job interview that Thomasina conducted two weeks earlier, sitting at a table close to where she and Atlas stood, came back to mind. "Do you know a woman named Sigma?" asked Thomasina.

"What if I do?"

Thomasina had not heard from Sigma since her brief protest, with fifteen like-minded malcontents in tow, the morning after that interview. "Were you among Sigma's friends massing outside here two weeks ago?" asked Thomasina.

"I've been in Alabama," answered Atlas, "staying over after a socialist party conference."

"Who would have thought it?" smiled Thomasina, in a joke private to herself.

A whole conversation was becoming private to Thomasina, quite different to the public one played out for Atlas staring at her and the barman still waiting behind the counter. The barmaid paused from watching them each time she served a customer. Those customers then watched Thomasina and Atlas from where

136

they stood or from stools or chairs on which they sat. Other customers were no longer talking among themselves or even looking in any direction. They watched Atlas and Thomasina.

"There are working class people here; my father among them," Thomasina told Atlas. "Aren't socialists supposed to help working classes?"

"You're not aware."

"I'm aware of my family, my countries…."

"I'm aware of justice."

"Do you go looking for people to offend you?" asked Thomasina. "Did Sigma or someone else tell you what happened here two weeks ago and you came here, all the way from Alabama, determined to be offended?"

"This is a free country," said Atlas.

"I don't want the freedom to go looking for people to offend me."

"You don't understand justice."

"Do you?"

Atlas turned back to the barman still watching her, before looking back at Thomasina. "I demand my beer," said Atlas, standing a little upright, in so far as she could, "or you'll be in trouble."

Thomasina turned to the barman. "You get back to the customers," she told him. "I'll deal with this."

"Can you pour beer?" Atlas asked her.

"I do when we're busy," answered Thomasina, "or short staffed."

Atlas looked around them. The barman was pouring a glass of beer for a customer. The barmaid was collecting an empty glass from a table. Thomasina's elderly father was at a table, no longer reading his newspaper but watching Thomasina and Atlas, as by then most of the customers were. There was something rather gratifying about her father not becoming involved, as he would have done when Thomasina was younger and would do again if he needed to.

"Are you busy now?" Atlas asked Thomasina.

"I'm dealing with you."

"You can't refuse me service because of my gender identity, or my sexual orientation."

Thomasina hadn't considered Atlas' sexual preferences. She

didn't want to. "I'm not refusing you service for either of those reasons," insisted Thomasina. "I'm refusing you service because you're obnoxious."

"You're obnoxious."

Thomasina thought of asking Atlas to leave, but wouldn't encourage her to feel any more the heroic victim than she already did. "You're free to go."

"Go, and give you the satisfaction of driving me out, like Sigma?"

"I never drove Sigma out," countered Thomasina. "If she'd wanted to buy anything then, or if she wanted to buy something now, we'd serve her."

Atlas stood staring at Thomasina. Thomasina stared at Atlas. Eventually, Atlas spoke up. "I want you to bake me a cake in honor of my transition," said Atlas.

"We don't bake cakes," answered Thomasina. "We're a pub and eatery." Thomasina looked around. By then, all the customers were staring at the two of them, as were all employees not otherwise engaged.

"I want a cake," demanded Atlas. "I want my beer and I want my cake."

Thomasina looked back at Atlas. "Did you come all the way from Alabama to demand a cake from a place that doesn't bake cakes?"

"You're making more trouble for yourself," said Atlas, her head bouncing up and down, "a lot more trouble than that brave protest two weeks ago. I'm sorry I missed it."

Bravery, like beauty, must be in the eyes of the beholder, thought Thomasina. "You would have enjoyed it," said Thomasina, as she might speak amicably of something worthwhile.

"Those sissies ran away when you threatened them," complained Atlas. "I don't run away."

"I can see that," said Thomasina, starting to enjoy their discourse more than she'd enjoyed any other since the interview she gave Sigma. "You might fall over."

"Are you shaming me?"

"Do you feel ashamed?"

"I never feel shame."

"Then I can't be shaming you, can I?"

Atlas stood silently for a moment, before speaking with less conviction than she normally spoke. "That doesn't sound right," she said, looking away. "I am what I feel."

"You mustn't feel well."

Atlas looked back up at Thomasina, finding her resolve again. "We have lawyers supporting us," insisted Atlas, her head bouncing up and down more so than ever before, "lawyers who believe in equality, freedom, and justice."

"Do you have chefs supporting you?"

Atlas reached down to the floor beside her, where stood a black canvas bag that Thomasina hadn't previously noticed. From the top of what seemed a stash of black clothes, Atlas picked up a small black camera facing up, from which protruded a suddenly obvious black microphone. Atlas held the unit close to her face, pointed at Thomasina. "You should know I've recorded everything since I came here," said Atlas. "I still am."

Thomasina smiled for the camera. She raised her hands and brushed up the curls in her hair.

Atlas turned, trailing the camera lens around the people watching her, her eyes remaining on the small screen capturing the images being recorded. Since Thomasina last looked, the kitchen staff had come out from the kitchen to watch. Nobody flinched to be filmed.

When she'd turned full circle, Atlas and her camera lens again faced Thomasina. "I'm giving you one more chance," said Atlas. "I want you to serve me the beer your barman refused to serve me. I want you to bake me a cake in honor of my gender transition: from female to male."

Thomasina thought of saying nothing. She thought of simply wishing Atlas a good day. She did neither of those things. "We are not serving you beer because you are rude to my staff," Thomasina told Atlas, her elocution particularly clear for the recording. "My cakes, I buy from bakeries. What taverns do you know that bake cakes?"

Atlas continued filming, until she would have been certain that Thomasina had nothing more to say. "Would anyone else like to say something?" she called out around the pub, her eyes remaining on the tiny electronic screen as the lens again panned around her audience. "Do you want to say this business should serve me a beer irrespective of my gender identity and sexual orientation? Do you want to say it should bake me a cake to support my sexuality and gender, or will you let your silence be your support for prejudice?"

Nobody answered. Customers and staff watched silently. None smiled at the camera, so far as Thomasina saw. Nor did they turn away. They simply stared without response at the camera recording them.

When she'd again turned full circle, Atlas returned her camera to her bag and picked up her bag. She turned to the front door and walked towards it, passing a table at which a man and woman sat watching her, with partly eaten meals on their plates and partly drunk glasses of wine. At their table, near to where Atlas walked, was an empty chair. Atlas kicked the chair over, jarring the man and woman back in their seats.

Atlas continued walking onto the door, which she opened. She then departed, leaving the door open behind her.

Thomasina walked to the fallen chair. She picked it up and placed it neatly back by the table. "I am sorry about that," she told the man and woman. "Can we get you anything more to eat or drink?"

She couldn't. She closed the entrance door.

Customers and staff continued watching Thomasina, checking that customers didn't need anything more and that employees didn't need her. Slowly, those customers returned to their conversations and musings, now about the short fat woman in black demanding a glass of beer and a cake. When customers and staff didn't need her, Thomasina slumped on an empty chair at the table at which her father, Salvatore, sat.

Salvatore stood up, slipped over to the bar, and soon returned with a glass of orange juice he gave her. He then sat back in his chair.

"You can be sure," Salvatore told Thomasina, "this isn't over." He would have seen and heard everything.

"Should I have let her buy a glass of beer?" asked Thomasina, before drinking her orange juice.

"You can't indulge customers screaming at your staff," he advised her, as he would. "If she apologized to the bartender, or if she apologizes to him now, then we can serve her."

Thomasina laughed. "What would she think to hear us calling her a woman?"

Salvatore smiled, too old and dignified ever to laugh. "She'd enjoy feeling offended without admitting she enjoyed it, even to herself. She'd enjoy even more demanding we call her a man."

For the rest of that day and the next, Thomasina glanced at every new customer entering the pub to see if it was Atlas, or Sigma, or someone else like them. Employees were asked to let Thomasina know immediately if Atlas returned. If Thomasina was not in the pub when Atlas returned, they should call her. Nobody did.

Many of the men in the pub and eatery wore suits, so there was nothing untoward about the man in the dark brown suit, carrying a matching dark brown briefcase, walking around the pub late Friday afternoon. He was middle-aged with unapologetically graying hair cut almost as short as Atlas' hair had been, and more than a little overweight as men of that age could be. Most importantly, he was obviously a man, without acting as anything else.

Thomasina noticed him because she noticed everyone there. Visitors were free to explore, looking around at the wall decorations or watching people playing pool on the pool table, without anyone bothering them. Only if they appeared lost, bewildered, or otherwise in need of assistance, were any of the staff to approach them.

He approached Thomasina. "Are you the manager?" he asked her.

Not wearing the staff uniform while moving freely behind the bar and out again must have made her appear like she was. "I am the manageress," she told him.

He offered her a business card she'd not previously noticed in his hand. "My name is Uri Peskin," he told her, "attorney at law."

Several lawyers were among the customers of the pub. None of them introduced themselves to Thomasina like that. Thomasina took his card.

"Do you have a lawyer?"

"Do I need one?"

"I represent Atlas Whalan."

Thomasina looked towards the table at which her father sat, talking with a customer but watching Thomasina. Her father said something to the customer, who went to another table.

That was his cue for her to sit the lawyer with him, if she wanted to do so. Her watching him without doing so was her cue for him to join them.

He did, after picking up his tweed cap from the table. Upon

reaching them, she gave him the business card she'd been given. "This is Atlas Whalan's lawyer," she told him.

"And you are?" Uri asked him.

Thomasina answered. "This is my father, Salvatore D'Amato," she told him. "He owns this place."

"Is there somewhere we can talk, Mister D'Amato," asked the lawyer, "Ms. D'Amato?"

"Miss D'Amato," Thomasina corrected him, "or Mrs. Vecoli."

"I prefer calling women Ms."

"I prefer being called Mrs. or Miss."

She picked up a leather folder from the bar counter, without thought of ordering anything from the menu inside it. The staff knew not to offer food or drinks to Thomasina or her father hosting meetings when they'd not asked for them beforehand. They hadn't.

Salvatore placed his tweed cap on his head, as Thomasina led the three of them through the pub and an external rear door to the patio deck. In the unpleasant company in which she and her father stepped, the salty breeze against her face was uncommonly refreshing.

Salvatore's cap was no protection from the breeze or the sun. They weren't the reasons he wore it, every time he stepped outside.

An extended roof sheltered the outdoor counter, where the beer faucets and other amenities were idle. That afternoon, the only patrons were seagulls overhead, sometimes squawking in conversations more meaningful than the one Thomasina and her father were about to endure.

Uri paused to stand looking across the street behind the pub towards the Atlantic Ocean, although he probably couldn't see anything above the levee. "You can't turn back the tide," he remarked, as if imparting something wise.

"Tides turn back naturally," Thomasina corrected him.

Anybody walking along that street could see them, but were unlikely to look. Anybody driving was even less likely to do so. Thomasina and her father were as good as alone with their unwelcome guest.

Thomasina led them sitting at a worn wooden table with a similarly worn bench along each side. Uri sat facing the rear of the pub, with his briefcase upright on the bench beside him. Thomasina and then Salvatore settled onto the bench facing the levee, with Uri obstructing their view.

Uri spoke first. "I have watched my client's video," he told them.

Thus, thought Thomasina, he had known she was the manageress. "Can't you understand my staff thinking that Atlas is a woman," she asked Uri, "not a lady, granted, but a woman?"

"My client wants to help you," he assured them, in a strangely kind and courteous manner. "I'm not here to punish, but to teach."

Thomasina might have been just as kind, but she wasn't nearly so courteous. "Your client could help herself by acquainting herself with reality," she told him.

Uri smiled. "I should pick you up for referring to him in the feminine, Ms. Vecoli. We call it misgendering."

"We call it telling the truth," responded Thomasina. "Should I pick you up for not referring to me as Mrs. Vecoli, or Miss D'Amato?"

Thomasina's father remained quiet, as he normally did the few occasions she'd invited him to business meetings. He would speak when it was in her interests he do so.

Uri resumed, occasionally looking at Salvatore. "Why can't you enjoy the infinity of available genders?" he asked Thomasina.

A dollop of bird dropping struck the tabletop between them. Thomasina glanced up at the seagulls.

Uri continued addressing Thomasina. "Why can't you enjoy the endless sexualities on offer," he asked, "when you stop thinking you're the only person who's normal? Join us in progress."

"This isn't progress," answered Thomasina. "It's not even regression, because that would mean we used to think like this. It's decay."

Uri shook his head. "We're not going to let America go backwards," he told her, "because you haven't come with us on our journey."

In the silence between them, the sounds of sea breeze and seagulls remained. Out of Thomasina's sight, people called to each other on the beach.

"You have a kitchen," resumed Uri. "You have chefs. You can bake gender-transition cakes."

"We don't bake cakes," answered Thomasina, offering Uri the leather folder she'd brought with her from inside the pub.

Uri took it and opened it to see two sheets of paper, on which were printed the eatery menu. Uri spent long enough reading it for Thomasina to think he might order something, before he closed the folder and laid it back on the table.

"We don't bake Peking Duck," resumed Thomasina, "Peruvian Horseradish, or cakes."

"What is Peruvian Horseradish?"

"Whatever it is, we don't bake it, fry it, or fricassee it. We don't bake, fry, or fricassee cakes."

"But you could, with your kitchen and chefs, bake Peking Duck, Peruvian Horseradish, if we knew what Peruvian Horseradish was, or cakes. Don't you want to earn money?"

"You refuse to run naked down the street for money," answered Thomasina, "even though you could."

"I'm not refusing," retorted Uri. "Are you willing to pay my hourly fees, including preparation time and time to redress afterwards?"

"I can't afford your hourly fees."

Uri turned to the oldest person at the table. "What do you think, Mister D'Amato?"

"I can't afford your fees."

Uri continued staring at him, while Salvatore turned to his daughter beside him. If she wanted him not to say anything more, not to engage in the meeting at that point, she should say something. She didn't.

Salvatore looked back at Uri. "When your type started blatantly lying," said Salvatore, "I thought you were testing us: seeing if the loudest, most persistent voices could persuade people of anything. You did. You then expanded your experiment. With every new pronouncement patently more preposterous than the last, like saying homosexuality was normal, I kept thinking that would be it: that surely we wouldn't believe this one, but we did. Changing gender should have been finally our moment to resist, but we didn't. I've stopped thinking there's a limit to what people believe, but people believing two is three, red is blue, night is day, doesn't make them true."

Thomasina wanted to seem cool and not react, but she could not help but smile. If Uri saw her smile, then she didn't care.

Salvatore continued. "Your talk is malarkey," he told Uri. "Gender diversity stops at two, and we don't decide which one is ours. Anything else is lunacy. Sexual diversity stops at one.

Anything else is perversion: sad for everyone concerned. People busily demanding we believe what they insist we believe can't see the pain left unanswered and the pain that they're causing. What's the joy of madness in a padded cell, drugged or not? Thinking we're in heaven doesn't leave us any less in hell."

Uri leant back in his bench, as if ready to give up and leave. "You're out of your mind," he told Salvatore.

"You think there's something exciting about gender dysphoria and sexual depravity," continued Salvatore, "but I'm out of my mind?"

"There's something arrogant about thinking you're right when nobody else does: nobody with my education."

"There's something stupid about thinking you're right because the nutcases around you think that you are."

Uri looked at Thomasina. If he wanted her to contradict her father, then she wouldn't, not publicly and not about that.

Salvatore continued answering Uri. "You think my family is unique," said Salvatore, "but since your client's friend almost three weeks ago and then your client this week collected so much attention here, I've had customers complain to me of their experiences of people deluded about gender and the love that goes with it. Some of them, I asked. Others took their chance to tell me. This country never feels closer than it feels to hear honest, rational people, caring about my daughter and me as we care about them. It never feels more divided than it feels to hear your client ranting at our barman for being polite, then bringing you here, like this, as if we're the problem."

"Who are these people who fail to grasp our modern understanding?" Uri demanded to know.

"Two Pennsylvania toyshop proprietors know boys and girls are different. A Connecticut library patron tried to keep a transvestite away from children, while a Boy Scouts leader from Washington State also provided moral leadership. All a West Virginian Girl Scout wanted was to grow up and raise a family; she'd have liked the Louisianan who helped his daughter flaunt her feminine beauty. An Iowa family felt driven from Rhode Island for knowing that people can't change gender, while a young Virginian woman stopped coaching girls' handball because a boy insisted upon playing. A young man from Maryland insists his girlfriends be girls."

Uri remained staring at Salvatore, with all his self-assurance in cross examination. "Are these people real?" asked Uri.

"Are you?"

"Where are they now?" asked Uri. "If you can't stand them before me, then I'll know that you're lying."

"If I stood them before you and they repeated to you what they told me," answered Salvatore, "you would accuse them of lying. If they produced witnesses to their testaments, you would accuse those witnesses of lying."

Uri remained unfazed. "All your conversationalists could stand at your side," he told Salvatore, "and you'd still have merely twelve ignorant bullies, from a country numbering in the hundreds of millions. I don't know anyone like you, not one. Get with the age, old timer."

That insult, and it was meant to be an insult, caught Thomasina's attention. It wasn't really an insult.

Her father became unusually animated, moving his arms and hands about as he spoke. "Would we be any less right if there were only twelve of us?" he asked Uri, his voice lifting. "Would I be any less right if there was only one of me, if the rest fled America for places where morality is normal: with only two genders and love between them?" Living beside an ocean meant the rest of the world could feel rather close: a single boat ride away, over the horizon.

"Where's that?" demanded Uri. "Where's the place that thinks like you think? It's not Canada; I have friends in Canada. It's not Britain, France, or Germany."

"It's Eastern Europe..."

"I wouldn't live there."

"It's Asia and Africa. It's every little island nation..."

"It's not Australia or New Zealand."

"They're big islands."

"What is it with you and backwards places?" asked Uri. "What would any of them know about the experiences of sexually and gender diverse people?"

"Your diverse people wouldn't be diverse if they understood normality," insisted Salvatore. "Normal people give us social contexts, societies, and we need societies more than we need anything else."

"We don't want your society," scoffed Uri. "You'd oppress millions of people."

"I'd liberate them," said Salvatore. "Rebuilding society would mean perversions fall away because we're connected to ever-widening circles of family; where parents stay together and stay with their children because they're parents; where those children grow up to become parents because that's what people do. We're each one of two genders and two is all we need. We each desire the other because only the other lets us build families."

"You're preaching…"

"Aren't you, but all you hear are people reading the same script, so you don't realize you're preaching? Let us be us, believing people who care about us instead of people who don't. There's no more certain way to destroy a people than to deny us descendants: to damn us with delusions of diversity."

Their table fell silent, as silent as it could be with seagulls squawking above. When Uri had no more reason to think he could persuade Salvatore or Thomasina to his point of view, there remained Atlas Whalan. Uri's voice slowed to something forceful and deliberate, but measured with the authority of a man empowered. "My client will sue you and your business for millions of dollars," he told Salvatore and Thomasina, his eyes moving between them. "You should notify your insurance company."

Thomasina responded for her and her father. "We're not paying extra insurance premiums for years to come, so you can earn legal fees on contingency and your mobsters can feel like they've won something."

Uri smiled, in the longest, most self-satisfied smile he'd shown. "Word of this case will bring donations for my fees from across the country," he assured her. "I don't work on contingency."

"We'll raise money from the last of the good people to fight you," said Thomasina. "I'll publish the stories of people my father mentioned."

Uri shook his head. "They will get every bit of the shellacking you will."

Thomasina smiled. "You would know about changing names to protect the innocent as much as the guilty, including you," she told Uri, with a little knowledge about what was ahead of her. "This won't be a case for depositions."

Uri rested his elbows on the table. His hand rested near his mouth, much as Thomasina's people once prayed.

Thomasina resumed. "I'll never stop saying I refused your client service because she was rude, and I'm thinking a jury of ordinary people will share my assessment. I'll never stop saying that we've never baked cakes, do not bake cakes, and will never bake cakes for anything or anyone. When your client loses the case and your mobsters don't win anything, however great they feel about themselves for fighting it, all people will have seen is money going to you. How many times can you come back to the trough?"

Uri pulled his arms from the table. He took hold of the handle of his briefcase beside him.

"None of that will save me from annoyance now," continued Thomasina, "but eventually the cases will stop, because people will have had enough of it all."

Uri's eyes speared at hers. "The money for our fight won't cease," he assured her, starting to stand. "You might win the case, but the case will outlast your business." His eyes and forehead motioned towards the rear of the pub, behind Thomasina and her father. "Because of our allegations against you, a thousand people who've never seen your place will publish scathing reviews of the food, service, and décor as if they'd suffered them all. You'll have your sympathizers, but too few of them willing to stick their necks out to save you. With all the other taverns about, customers close enough to step through your open door won't risk your sullied place. Your critics will muddy your reputation so much, not even the rats will come."

"This case isn't about me," declared Thomasina.

Uri smiled. "Of course, it isn't about you, your father, or your salty pub," he said, rising from his bench, his potent briefcase in hand. "People far from here, who've never met you but who might think like you, will see your life consumed with this case. They'll learn to respect people's genders and orientations so it doesn't happen to them, until every American does. Whether Atlas Whalan sues you or I focus on another case to wage, you're just another skirmish in a war we're going to win."

With the assurance in his step that victors enjoyed, Uri stepped around the bench and away. He proceeded through the space in the wooden fence to the street.

Thomasina and her father remained at the table. The ocean was loud, overwhelming any sounds from people playing on the beach. Seagulls remained overhead, still squawking.

"Will they win?" Thomasina asked her father. "All we do is talk and listen."

Salvatore smiled, in a smile gentler than any she'd seen from Uri. "*Tesoro*," he said, "let me tell you about two women and their fiancés visiting the Jersey Shore, one couple from California and one from Washington..."

11 THE LATE MISTER CRIMPTON

Old America had been a time of patience, savoring time and all that time afforded, most notably time for love. Few experiences afforded men and women more time to fall in love than travelling great distances.

Those travelers included passengers aboard the British ocean liner *Queen Mary*, plying the North Atlantic from 1936 to 1967. After her retirement, the old lady was permanently moored at Long Beach, California. While America became impatient and air travel became the means to get to places quickly, the *Queen Mary* remained a hotel, museum, and site for shops and dining. Its decks and stairs played host to film crews filming scenes set aboard old ships, with covered lifeboats at the ready.

Most importantly, for Paisley Lambeth two decades into the twenty-first century, no local venue for live music offered a better outlook, while patrons ate and drank. Early Thursday evening, she sat with Miriam Fleischer across a table in the Observation Bar, drinking from glasses of Pina Colada. Beside them were the distant lights of Long Beach, shining above still water. The band would soon start playing.

Both women were aged about twenty-five. They were much alike in their average female heights and figures, although Miriam's low-heeled leather shoes left her a little shorter than Paisley, with her longer-heeled leather shoes.

Their clothes and hairstyles couldn't have been more different. Miriam's black hair she wore short, as she instructed her hairdresser to cut it each time she saw him. Paisley's thick blonde hair flowed onto her shoulders, less curtailed by her female hairdresser. Miriam wore suits, with collared shirts and matching ties. Paisley wore slacks in various shades of dark, with paler blouses open enough to reveal her neck and nothing more.

Their only wear in common was their tortoiseshell glasses: imitation tortoiseshell, as tortoiseshell glasses had become. Their glasses matched, although Miriam wore thicker heavyset frames, in spite of her face and bone structure being no heavier set than Paisley's. They'd met through friends three months earlier.

"My mother telephoned me today," said Paisley, preparing to sip her Pina Colada. "She only ever telephones me for a reason, but she found out this morning from his widow that our next-door neighbor Mister Crimpton died three weeks ago." Paisley's mother hadn't seen Mrs. Crimpton for several months when she saw her at her letterbox that morning.

"You've never mentioned him," responded Miriam.

"I have thought about him," said Paisley, "many too many times." Paisley reached her hand across the table, taking Miriam's hand in hers. "I've been thinking about him ever since my mother called."

Miriam smiled. "He must be the only man you ever think about."

Paisley pulled back her hand. "I wish I didn't think of any men."

It was St Valentine's Day, and a young woman moved from table to table with a basket selling long-stemmed roses in clear plastic cylinders. She stopped at the table at which Paisley and Miriam sat. "Would you like something for your boyfriends," she asked them, "or husbands?"

"I will never have a boyfriend!" snapped Miriam, "or a husband!"

The young woman stepped back. She then proceeded to the next table.

Paisley and then Miriam laughed. Paisley didn't feel the need to tell everyone she met as much as Miriam told everyone she met, but what was true of Miriam was no less true of Paisley.

Saturday morning, Paisley visited her mother, as she normally only did for her mother's birthday or Thanksgiving. Divorced for many years, her mother still lived in what had been Paisley's girlhood home: a comfortable bungalow along Argonne Avenue, where the curtains were always open and daytime bright.

Instead of talking, Paisley stood at the lounge room window, looking through her tortoiseshell glasses over the flowers and fence at as much as she could see of the Crimpton house above them. The Crimpton house was much alike her girlhood home in its ordinary appearance, but appearances could deceive. Its curtains were normally closed.

Somewhere close behind her was her mother. "I wasn't certain if you remembered Mister Crimpton," her mother said. "We never saw as much of our neighbors as my sister and her family do in Albuquerque."

Paisley remembered Mister Crimpton. He had been a large man, with a large face and girth. He was decidedly unattractive, through the years Paisley saw him, so much so it seemed extraordinary he ever married. His wife was plain and unassuming, so perhaps undemanding in the man she married. She would have had to be undemanding to marry Mister Crimpton.

Her mother resumed. "In all the years I've lived here," she said, "I don't think anything about the Crimpton house ever changed. I've not changed my home, our home, very much, but I laid that new front path and planted new bushes where I could. I don't think Mister or Mrs. Crimpton ever did anything. I can't see Mrs. Crimpton doing anything now, unless Mister Crimpton was her reason for leaving everything as it was."

Paisley turned around to face her mother. "How often would you have seen Mister Crimpton?" asked Paisley.

Her mother was sitting in an armchair with a cup of tea. Another cup of tea sat on a saucer on the small table.

"Ooh," her mother answered, "I can't really say."

"When I was young, say ten years old, how often did you see him?"

"Why would you ever want to know such a thing?"

"Please..."

Paisley's mother took a moment to think of her answer. "We never socialized together," she answered, "unlike my sister with her neighbors in Albuquerque."

"Did you talk," asked Paisley, "along the sidewalk, at their letterbox, at ours?"

"I talked with Mrs. Crimpton when I saw her, and I must have spoken with Mister Crimpton sometime. I can't remember when."

Paisley took the tea her mother had prepared. She sat in the armchair facing her, without drinking from it.

Her mother resumed their conversation. "I can't remember you ever asking about Mister Crimpton, before today," she said.

"I did ask you," said Paisley. "I was ten years old, when you found me in my bedroom. I asked you what you thought of him, and you told me you thought he was very nice. You said we should try to spend more time with our neighbors."

Paisley's mother shook her head. "How can you remember a conversation from fifteen years ago?"

"I remember everything from fifteen years ago," answered Paisley. "I remember the aroma of grass freshly cut in his front yard. I remarked to him upon you mowing our lawn, producing the same aroma. I remember the smell of his thick after-shave lotion, so pungent aside the perfumes you wore. I remember the stutter that crept into his voice."

Paisley's mother sat silently, watching her daughter. Paisley looked back and forth around the room, most often at the window beyond which stood the Crimpton home. Every time her eyes returned to her mother, her mother was watching her.

The house beyond the window haunted her, much as it had since she was ten years old, even after moving to her apartment when she was eighteen years of age. Never could Paisley imagine returning there while Mister Crimpton was in residence, but Mister Crimpton no longer was, unless he haunted that house much as he haunted every other.

Paisley stood up. She returned her cup and saucer, from which she'd not drunk any tea, to the table. "I'm going outside," she said, walking from the room.

Soon, Paisley stood on the sidewalk outside the Crimpton home. Ahead of her, beyond the gate, was a concrete path unchanged since Paisley first saw it. The house was quiet, the grass overgrown. A mower from a nearby lawn sounded through the air, but not from the Crimpton yard.

Whether approaching the house would teach Paisley anything, she didn't know. She knew it wouldn't hurt her, as she'd not known when Mister Crimpton was alive, not since she was ten years old.

Mrs. Crimpton might not be there, but Paisley knew she would be. She'd not gone anywhere when Mister Crimpton was alive and she probably wasn't about to start.

Opening the gate, leaving it open, Paisley approached the house. She knocked on the front door, and waited.

Finally, the door opened, revealing Mrs. Crimpton staring at her. She too was overweight, but that was no reason not to like her as her late husband having been overweight was another reason to dislike him.

"I'm Paisley Lambeth," she said. "I used to live next door."

Resignation slipped through Mrs. Crimpton's face, making her first words to Paisley all the more surprising. "I'm glad you came."

Mrs. Crimpton stepped back, inviting Paisley inside. What would have been frightening from Mister Crimpton was strangely unaffecting from Mrs. Crimpton.

"You never used to wear glasses," observed Mrs. Crimpton, behind her.

The Crimptons' lounge room was familiar, from Paisley's last visit there when she was ten years old. The room was dark, with curtains obscuring most of the light through the windows. It was all extraordinarily bland, but for the gaunt young blond-haired man of about Paisley's age, less like a man than a boy, sitting in a sofa, his legs together, his arms at his side, his hands clasped together on his lap. Brown braces he probably didn't need to wear held up his thin trousers.

"Do you remember Jerome Thripp?" Mrs. Crimpton asked Paisley. "He used to live with his mother on the other side of our home from you. His mother still lives there, like your mother in your home. People living in Argonne Avenue don't ever want to leave, do we?"

Paisley had wanted to leave Argonne Avenue. She had wanted to leave since she was ten years old.

She did not remember Jerome. She did not remember anyone from the neighborhood, except the Crimptons.

"Can I make you some tea?" Mrs. Crimpton asked Paisley. "Can I get you some cookies?"

"I'm not thirsty," answered Paisley. "I'm not hungry."

"Would you like to sit down?"

Paisley sat in a single chair, spread as far from Mrs. Crimpton in another armchair and Jerome in the sofa as the three could be in that room. Jerome studied Paisley, from a distance much more than the seven or eight feet between them.

Mrs. Crimpton started the conversation. "Jerome has visited me often in the weeks since Mister Crimpton died," she told Paisley.

Uninterested in sociable conversation, untroubled by the stranger with them, Paisley blurted out her words at Mrs. Crimpton. "Do you know what Mister Crimpton did?" she asked.

Mrs. Crimpton looked back at her. She looked at Jerome. She looked back at Paisley. "I know," she said.

Paisley hadn't really heard her answer. "After I talked to him from the sidewalk about the lovely smell of freshly mown grass," Paisley explained, as she'd never before said to anyone, "he offered me candy. My mother never gave me candy, so why wouldn't I accept? He brought me in here."

She looked around the room, to know again it was the room. It remained unchanged, as caves and hell did.

"He said that you were out shopping for groceries," Paisley continued. "He said that he always liked me." She looked at the sofa on which Jerome sat; Jerome was so inconsequential to the moment, Paisley didn't care what he learnt. "There," she pointed her hand and index finger towards the sofa, with Mrs. Crimpton still in a corner of her sight, "he touched me, as no person ever had before and no man has again."

Mrs. Crimpton dropped her head, facing her lap. Jerome remained sitting.

Instead of Mrs. Crimpton, Jerome spoke up. His voice was soft, more feminine than masculine. "I was eleven years old," said Jerome, slowly drawing Paisley's attention to him, "when I noticed him trimming the grass along the edges of the path; I'd never known before today how often he must have tended to his lawns. My mother didn't trim the grass. She mowed the lawns, until I was old enough to mow them, but she did as little as she could around our home and so did I. Our yard was never as nice as the Crimptons' yard or any other yards, which might have irked our other neighbors but who worried about them?"

Sometime since he'd started speaking, Jerome stopped looking at Paisley. He looked through her, much as she'd once looked through him.

"He told me that Mrs. Crimpton was at the dentist and would not return home until late," continued Jerome, "when he offered me gingerbread men from his kitchen. I never had treats at home and whoever had gingerbread away from Christmastime? I had gingerbread rarely enough then. In this sofa, with the front door locked and window curtains closed, he gave me gingerbread. He told me that he always liked me, which no person ever before had. He must have liked both of us."

The silence lingered. For the first time since she'd heard of Mister Crimpton's death, and for an interminable time before then, Paisley wasn't thinking about herself.

Jerome resumed his recollection, more comprehensive than Paisley's had been. "My father left my mother and me before I was old enough to remember," said Jerome, "so when Mister Crimpton took such an interest in me as I'd never before known, I was overjoyed. He touched me with love – I thought it was love – which no person before had. From out of nowhere, all of a sudden, I had a loving father. He was my mother's loving husband – my loving husband – in my empty, broken mind."

In his glazed blue eyes, Paisley looked for signals of an emotion preparing to burst forth. None came, but nor had they come from her.

"When Mister Crimpton finished," resumed Jerome, "he called my experience our little secret. I've spent my life trying to get those feelings again as I got from Mister Crimpton."

His eyes found focus upon Paisley. She thought again about herself.

"I never revealed to anyone what happened before revealing it to Mrs. Crimpton," he confided, "coming here much as you've done, after I'd learned that he died. Since then, I've sat here with Mrs. Crimpton every day and night I could, repeating every thought and feeling in my hope I'd eventually lose interest."

Paisley's experience of Mister Crimpton was not unique, when she'd always presumed it was. Her first reaction to it might have been. "I think I hate all men because of him," she confided in Jerome. Mrs. Crimpton had become as unimportant as Jerome had previously been. "If he could do that to me, then all men could. Even if they wouldn't, they let him do it."

"So," said Jerome, "you've never had a boyfriend?" He laughed, in as unconvincing a laugh as Paisley had ever heard. "I've never had a girlfriend."

Paisley turned back to Mrs. Crimpton. "Who came to Mister Crimpton's funeral?" asked Paisley.

"There was no funeral. He hated religion and ritual, and the only person who would have come would have been me."

"Did you know what he did?" asked Paisley, again.

"He was weak," answered Mrs. Crimpton, "but he knew he was weak. Mister Crimpton cried his confession to me of what he'd done to each of you, crying like the baby we never had for an hour or more. Week after week, he'd break into tears again, all around the house. Some mornings, he called in sick to work because he knew he'd be crying that day, crying for you and for himself. I think he also cried for me, that I should be party to it all."

"Why you?" asked Paisley.

"We'd tried but been unable to have children. I became very sick, and didn't want him touching me. I should never have been a wife, not with Mister Crimpton. I insisted that he sleep in a spare bedroom, one that would have been a room for children but children never came. That was when he put on weight, as I did.

"He said he never assaulted you two because he'd been assaulted as a boy, by his piano teacher, and he was careful to ensure that he was gentler than that with each of you. He called it love because people now think love is anything they want love to be, but I told him it wasn't love. I told him over and over again that love could only be between him and me, hugging him every time I said it, until he finally believed me."

"I can't forgive him," said Paisley.

"I don't think he forgave himself. We never shared a room or bed again, but he accepted his penance and was a little glad for it. I think he wanted to be punished." She looked at Jerome and back at Paisley. "You two were his only victims, if that comforts you. He never committed those atrocities again."

Paisley stood up; it was easier than thinking any more. She began to walk around the room, expending energy she could not otherwise expend.

She went to the sofa on which Jerome sat but away from him, facing the fabric where she'd sat fifteen years ago. She kicked the base of the sofa, but that was hard and it hurt her foot. Kneeling against the sofa, she began punching the cushions. She punched what might have been the cushion against which she'd sat fifteen years ago. She punched the cushion back-rest. She punched as she'd never before punched, as men not women punched. She punched wanting to break that sofa, but it didn't break. She continued punching.

She cried. She punched. She cried again. She tired, but it was good tired; she needed to be exhausted. She needed to vent everything until nothing remained to vent. Finally, she collapsed her hand against the cushion, still sobbing.

Slowly recovering her breath and mind, Paisley pushed herself back upright, looking away from Mrs. Crimpton and Jerome so they could not see her eyes. "When I was young," she said, "he was so big and I was small, but now I'm big enough, I see he wasn't very big. He's not menacing anymore; he can't hurt me anymore. If he were here now, I could kick and punch him. If that was not enough, I could run into his kitchen and take a carving knife with which I'd cut him up into bloody scraps."

Paisley wiped her cheeks dry with her finger. She dried the corners of her eyes, sniffling.

Silence followed. It was one for Mrs. Crimpton, behind Paisley, to break. "Managing his factory," she said, "Mister Crimpton was a respected man in the community, who should have known better. He knew much about many things, but he believed people thinking that he knew right from wrong. If they saw weakness in him, they never mentioned it, so he didn't know that it was there, until it took him. I only ask, or suggest, you try a little to understand him, not for his sake, nothing affects him now, but for yours."

Wanting to punch or kick him more, Paisley turned towards her. "Where do we find his grave?" she asked.

Mrs. Crimpton shook her head. "I didn't want to spend the rest of my life shuffling to a cemetery," she replied, "on his birthdays and our wedding anniversary. No one but I was ever going to visit him, so that after I died nobody would. He'd be one of those graves that people momentarily ponder as they wander near the graves of loved ones and soon forget. He was cremated so I could sprinkle his ashes on a rose bush behind our home. The only trips I'll have to make will be into our backyard."

"Show me," insisted Paisley.

Mrs. Crimpton led Paisley and Jerome through the house and out through a rear door, into a small yard more overgrown than the front yard. She led them to a row of rose bushes along the boundary at the rear of the property, and to one bush furthest to one side, by the fence over which was Paisley's girlhood home.

Around the base of the bush, the gray of ashes remained visible. If they made Mister Crimpton's life seem small, then they also made other lives seem small.

Paisley reached her shoe forward to the nearest ashes. She probably should have asked Mrs. Crimpton's permission before doing what she did, but she feared her not giving it. The sole of her shoe pressed down against the ashes, she ground them into the dirt, as she might have extinguished a flame before it could do any harm.

She continued grinding, scolding the dead man as she no longer could any other way. Her grinding became so furious, she held her tortoiseshell glasses for fear that they might fall. Mrs. Crimpton and Jerome said nothing, while Paisley ground away. She set about obliterating the residue of Mister Crimpton's life into the dirt no less surely than he'd once obliterated her life in that awful house behind her. Whether any residue of hers remained wasn't clear.

When she finished, Paisley pulled her foot and shoe away. She went to the grass and wiped the sole of her shoe there.

Paisley looked around until she saw a faucet, against the rear of the house. Leaving Mrs. Crimpton and Jerome behind, she went and turned it on, releasing that small torrent of clear water. Leaning against the house, balancing upon her other leg, she removed her shoe. Turning up the sole, she washed it.

She washed it long, dousing the sole and edges of her shoe with the risk that water might ruin them to be certain no trace of Mister Crimpton remained with her. When Paisley was certain she had washed every ash of him away, she washed her shoe again. Then, she returned her shoe to her foot. She turned off the faucet.

From several yards away, Mrs. Crimpton and Jerome had watched her. For a moment, Paisley stood watching them, wondering if she had anything more to ask or anything more to say or do there. She didn't, so she turned and made her own way back through the house, opening the front door and departing. Whether Mrs. Crimpton or Jerome had followed her, was not of her concern.

When Paisley returned to her mother's home, her mother was standing at her open front door. She stood back to let Paisley enter, return to the living room, and sit down in the same chair in which she'd sat earlier that day.

The front door closed behind her, Paisley's mother again sat in the chair in which she'd sat earlier that day. The cups of tea had gone. Only Paisley and her mother were there.

Paisley imagined her mother asking her where she had gone. She probably didn't want to intrude.

Silently they sat. That chair, that room, within sight through the window of Mister Crimpton's home (but no longer Mister Crimpton's home) was not a place to contemplate.

He couldn't hurt her there. No one had ever hurt her in that room or home as Mister Crimpton had hurt her in the corresponding home next door.

Whether Paisley felt better for the day, she wasn't sure. She certainly felt no worse. She had knowledge where previously she did not, which was probably good. She had no understanding of Mister Crimpton, although she probably should and didn't want to anyway. She was glad that he was dead, wishing only that he'd died sooner, more than fifteen years sooner, before she'd smelt the grass he'd cut.

She was also glad her mother saw Mrs. Crimpton to learn that he was dead. She was glad for the time she'd spent in Mrs. Crimpton's home.

Jerome had returned there time and time again. Paisley would not return. If she thought of a question to ask Mrs. Crimpton then she might return, but she would have no more questions.

As much of herself, she thought of Jerome. Striving to repeat his experience of Mister Crimpton had consumed his life. Striving to escape her same experience had consumed hers.

His response to Mister Crimpton seemed so crazy. Her response might also have been crazy. The only responses to craziness were crazy.

She couldn't help it. Could he? Could she?

Paisley couldn't tell her mother what happened that day any more than she could tell her what happened fifteen years earlier; it wasn't her place to do so, and she didn't want to talk about such things with people who'd not comprehend. She wouldn't mention them to Miriam, who would only use them to berate men without thought of Paisley, whatever thoughts of Paisley should be. She would not mention them to anyone again.

Her thoughts she'd already made, sitting there, Paisley made again. After an hour, she rose from her chair. Her mother watched her stand and turn away. They would talk again sometime, on her mother's birthday or at Thanksgiving, but not yet, although not about that day and not about the Crimptons. Silently, Paisley left her girlhood home, such as it was, her mother watching her go, closing the front door after her.

Again, Paisley saw the front of the Crimptons' home, without seeing anything about it kept within, or anybody there. Her eyes might have dwelt upon it, but no more or less than they'd dwelt upon it through her preceding visits.

She returned to her adult home, such as it was. Her adult home was boring, but boredom was very good. Paisley lay alone on her bed, remaining there throughout the afternoon, sometimes staring at the ceiling, sometimes not.

She didn't see Miriam that evening. She didn't see anyone. "Please, understand," she asked Miriam, as she asked her again every time Miriam wanted to see her through the ensuing weeks.

When she wasn't working, Paisley remained at home, thinking about Mister Crimpton and her life since she was ten years old, thinking about nothing. She thought about Jerome, and their vastly different reactions to the same provocation, from their vastly different vantages. He might also have been thinking about her because, almost three weeks after they'd met in Mrs. Crimpton's home, he called her.

He'd obtained Paisley's telephone number from her mother, who Paisley knew would have been delighted that a man was asking for it. Paisley smiled, amused; her mother didn't know of Jerome's relationships as Paisley knew.

Jerome wanted to talk. The simplest, safest, most obvious place to meet was the *Queen Mary*, but not the bar at which Paisley had sat with Miriam.

Late Saturday afternoon, Paisley waited on the sun deck towards the vessel's stern. The old timber and fixtures reminded her that the *Queen Mary* wasn't just a place for rendezvous, but of history, from a time long before Paisley was ten years old. Standing at a timber railing, she looked away from Long Beach, into the endless Pacific Ocean. Imagining the ship in service more than half a century earlier was easy, as if Paisley were headed somewhere distant.

From behind her, came a voice. "I've not been here before," he said.

Paisley turned to see Jerome standing on the deck, five or six feet from her. His voice was deeper than it had been, the only previous time they'd met. Instead of wearing braces, a belt held up his trousers, as belts did for other men. It also made Paisley conscious of how unusual her tortoiseshell glasses had become.

Other visitors on the deck were far enough away not to hear him. "After your visit," said Jerome, stepping towards her, "I continued visiting Mrs. Crimpton every chance I could." He spoke just loud enough for only Paisley to hear. "I think we're lucky to have Mrs. Crimpton believing us, telling us what she could."

Paisley did not feel lucky. She did not feel lucky at all.

"We talked of her and Mister Crimpton," continued Jerome. "I've still not talked with anyone else, not even my mother, about what happened to me fifteen years ago. I won't be telling anyone about what happened to you."

Neither had Paisley told anyone. Neither would she. The only three people alive who knew what happened to them fifteen years earlier would remain the only three.

"Most of all," said Jerome, "we talked of me, but we also talked of you. We kept hoping you'd return to see us if you needed to return, but most of all we hoped you didn't need to return."

Paisley leant back against the railing. Jerome took another step closer.

"She was right, Mrs. Crimpton," Jerome continued. "The love I thought Mister Crimpton gave me wasn't love. I've spent my life since then chasing more of it, but love was never what I thought love was."

His candor was the candor of the last time they'd seen each other. Candor could be the most vulnerable of honesty.

"I can't undo the past," said Jerome. "I can't undo Mister Crimpton, making him vanish from my history, but I don't think I want him to vanish. If my comfort from Mister Crimpton wasn't because of him but because of my feelings for my father, then they're more pain and longing I need not let disturb me. I can leave them both to history, I think."

Paisley did not know if she could. "I still hate Mister Crimpton," she said, thinking aloud and expressing her thoughts with the only person who might understand, in time, when she didn't understand herself. "He was the culprit, only him, but I also hate the piano teacher who abused him, without knowing who he was, because what he did to Mister Crimpton he did to me. If someone abused that piano teacher, then I'd hate that abuser too. I'd hate all the abusers who, along that fuse through time, abused me, but only the abusers. Is that strange of me, I'm not very sure?"

Jerome smiled. "I might be the expert in strange," he answered her, "but that fuse of yours and mine stops with us, if we stop it."

Pulling her back from the railing, Paisley stood upright, still facing him. "You and I shared an experience I wish neither of us had known," she said, "but we have. I don't know if that's a basis for a friendship; I haven't much experience of friendships, but I don't hate men anymore."

Jerome moved a little closer to her. She'd not been that close to a man, in such a personal situation, since Mister Crimpton.

"I don't love Miriam anymore," said Paisley, although Jerome couldn't know who Miriam was. "Whether that was ever really love, I'd need more time to comprehend, but I want us to keep being friends, if we can, if too much hasn't happened for us to be friends."

With the smallest of steps, Jerome stood close enough to touch her. She wavered, remaining there.

His right hand hanging by his side took her left hand. She hesitated with the touch, knowing that if she wanted him to pull away he would, but his touch was gentler than she'd have imagined a man's touch to be. It was nevertheless stronger than a woman's soft touch. Jerome seemed altogether stronger and more certain than he'd seemed that first time Paisley saw him: huddled on that sofa in Mrs. Crimpton's home.

Paisley slowly became comfortable. She removed her tortoiseshell glasses from her face, holding them in her free hand. She didn't need them to see. She'd never needed them to see.

Jerome's left hand took her right hand, releasing those glasses to fall down to the deck. They could fall out to the ocean and Paisley wouldn't mind. His hand holding hers was easier for Paisley the second time.

Their hands holding each other, Jerome's face leant towards her. Paisley watched him near her, as Jerome watched her eyes. Their eyes seeing only each other's eyes made everything sublime, her eyes closing as they kissed.

12 THE WOMEN'S CLUB

Chartered in 1821, George Washington University prided itself on many things, early in the twenty-first century. Being chartered in 1821 was no longer one of them.

Among its accomplishments, some said none was greater than the Elizabeth J Somers Women's Leadership Program. Certainly, some women said it, including Nell Somersby when she applied to join for her freshman year.

Not every application succeeds. Hers didn't, although Nell was accepted into the University to study communications at the Foggy Bottom Campus in the District of Columbia, near the National Mall. Thus in August, Nell left her Ohio family home to move to Washington and into a room on the second floor of eight at Mitchell Hall, at the south-east corner of the campus.

Hers was a single room, without a friend from home or anywhere else with whom to share. Some people made lifelong friends from their roommates at college, she knew, and Nell wanted to make friends, but she also knew that not all roommates became friends. There were other means of making friends at college.

Newly enrolled students already knew whatever technical details about courses they'd wanted to know, but beyond the folklore of films and television programs, they knew little about college life away from study (and not much about student life while studying). While other students had the curse or benefit of older siblings to frighten or console them, Nell was an eldest child. She would need to educate her younger brothers in two and four years' time, but that was for two and four years' time.

Before classes commenced, there was Orientation Week, or Welcome Week, on which Nell depended to learn something of the plethora of student groups and societies. Scattered among the open spaces inside buildings, and outside when the weather allowed it, stalls and tables offered members for freshmen students to meet, as well as pamphlets and papers for those students to take. A few even offered gifts of badges, pens, and the like.

While other students wore faded blue denim jeans, Nell wore a colorful long dress, her lively thick fair hair reaching to her back. More diligently than other students, she examined all the stalls that might be of interest to her, collecting one each of the offerings in her recyclable paper bag.

Nell stopped long enough at several stalls and tables to speak with the older students volunteering their time. When their words turned to conversation long enough, because other freshmen students didn't interrupt, Nell introduced herself to students only a year or two older than she was. They were all the wiser for those one or two years.

Older than most other students was the woman behind the table marked for the Women's Club, early that afternoon. Her hair was long, as much younger women wore it, but gray. She wore a woolen shawl, covering her arms and shoulders. Infrequently her hands appeared from beneath the shawl, before disappearing under it again.

The woman smiled at Nell. "Is this your first year?" she asked Nell. She was the first person Nell had encountered not to speak of first year students being freshmen.

Nell nodded. She had presumed all the students stopping at stalls and tables were freshmen.

"Is this your first time away from home?"

Again, Nell nodded. She'd left that home only a few days earlier, to return some weekends and at each break.

"What do you like most about G W?"

"I like being in Washington," answered Nell. "Places like the Lincoln Memorial I used to have to hurry about on vacations and school trips, now I can see any day I want to, just by walking a few blocks."

The woman behind the table again smiled. "Everything here is so international," she said. "I love it!"

"I'm Nell Somersby," she said, "from Cleveland."

The woman took a pen from the table and wrote Nell's name and the name of her hometown, at the foot of a list of thirty or so names and hometowns. "If you give me your email address, I can send you notices of our events," said the woman. "You're not obliged to come, and you can unsubscribe at any time."

Nell recited her electronic mail address. She watched the

woman carefully write it down, as people had to do with electronic mail.

When she finished writing, the woman put her pen down and looked up. "Zoe Phegyn," she introduced herself, "from Houston once, now Georgetown, Georgetown for a long time now, but I like to say Planet Earth."

"Not the Solar System?" smiled Nell, before hoping her words sounded as jovial as she'd intended them to be.

Zoe nodded. "Yes," she said. "No, wait…," she added, smiling, "the Universe!"

She stood up from her chair behind the table; she and Nell were roughly the same height. From beneath her shawl, Zoe reached out her arm to shake Nell's hand.

Nell wasn't accustomed to women shaking hands. She wasn't accustomed to anyone shaking her hand, but coming to college was becoming an adult. Her arms back under her shawl, Zoe sat back down.

"I've not been to Georgetown," said Nell. "I've been to Planet Earth," she smiled, "the Solar System, and the Universe, but not Georgetown."

"Georgetown's pretty," said Zoe, "without politicians and the corporations that pay them you find in most of Washington." She looked down at a glazed pottery mug in front of her on the table. "I bought this in Georgetown," she said, picking up the mug.

On the mug were artistic drawings of café chairs and windows, in the style of old French paintings. Nell liked art.

"A woman made it," said Zoe, bringing the mug to her mouth to drink before placing it back down. "Iced tea," she explained.

"When and where does the Women's Club meet?" asked Nell. She asked the same question of all the clubs and societies tempting her interest, and of those when someone had engaged her in conversation long enough for asking to be courteous.

"When and where I decide," smiled Zoe. "I always find us a room."

A young man appeared beside Nell. "I love women," he smiled, looking at Nell. "Does that qualify me for the Women's Club?"

He was of Nell's age, a little taller, and athletic, with closely cut blond hair. Among all those faded jeans around them, an uncommonly thick tan leather belt around his waist separated his white trousers from his pale striped cotton shirt.

"I'm sorry," interjected Zoe, drawing Nell's attention back to her, pointedly addressing her not the man. "We can't control who comes to our table, but we can control who comes to our meetings."

The man continued. "I can't think of any place I'd rather be than in a room full of beautiful women," he said, drawing Nell back to him, before glancing at Zoe and smiling back at Nell, "or with at least one beautiful woman."

Zoe, her voice raised a little, continued talking to Nell, as if the man wasn't there and as if Nell wasn't looking at him. "I've convened a social for first year students at six o'clock tonight," said Zoe.

Nell turned back to her. All Nell seemed to be doing was turning back and forth between them.

"At our socials," Zoe elaborated, "you can socialize with other students."

The man replied. "I'd be delighted," he said.

"No men admitted," answered Zoe.

Nell looked back at the man. "I am trying to make friends in Washington," she told him.

"May I audition?" he smiled. "I'm Randy Tulloch."

Zoe quipped, "You would be."

Nell didn't need to look to know that Zoe didn't pick up her pen. She didn't write Randy's name.

Nevertheless, Nell answered him. "I would like to attend the Women's Club social," she told him. "I want to see what it's like."

"I would too," said Randy, before looking at Zoe, "but I respect being told that I can't." He looked back at Nell. "For after your social," he told her, "a few of us are headed to Georgetown for burgers tonight."

"Zoe likes Georgetown," enthused Nell, "like her mug."

"I don't eat burgers," said Zoe.

Randy crouched down close to the table, studying Zoe's colorful mug. She pulled the mug away from him.

"The mug says Martin's," said Randy, standing up and again facing Nell. "That's Martin's Tavern," he told her. "Do you like root beer?"

Zoe answered, for Nell to hear. "We prefer coffee shops," said Zoe.

"I thought you might," smiled Randy, without looking at Zoe.

"I'm guessing something gluten free?"

That Nell was facing Randy didn't faze Zoe. "After our social," Zoe obviously told Nell, not Randy, "we can all go to one of my favorite coffee shops in Georgetown. I have several."

"I can do coffee shops," Randy told Nell. "I'd even eat lentils, if that's what you like."

Zoe answered him before Nell could. "We don't want your toxic masculinity," she told him.

Randy continued facing Nell. "Masculinity isn't toxic," he answered Zoe, before looking at Zoe. So did Nell. "Haven't you a boyfriend?"

"I'm not submitting my body to the patriarchy."

"You might like it."

Her face seized with the indignity, Zoe pulled back in her chair. Nell smiled, but knew she shouldn't.

"What are you studying?" Randy asked Zoe.

Zoe sat upright again. Nell expected her not to answer him, but she did. "I'm in the Women's, Gender, and Sexuality Studies Program," she said.

"Thought so," muttered Randy.

Nell addressed Zoe. "That's quite a mouthful."

"We're the oldest program of its kind in the United States," boasted Zoe. "Whatever you're studying, you can take some of our subjects."

Randy responded. "Do you get many students from Civil Engineering?"

Zoe glanced at Randy long enough to seem like she wasn't going to answer him. Again, she did. "Do we want any?"

"Guess not," he said, before looking back at Nell. "I'd submit my body to the matriarchy."

Another woman appeared at the table, looking at the pamphlets and papers. Zoe began speaking to her, as Randy and Nell faced each other. "I should try the Women's Club social," she told him. "After the coffee shop, I'll find Martin's Tavern."

Randy smiled. "I'll look out for you," he told her. "They say that President Kennedy proposed marriage to Jackie there."

Zoe responded. "That's of no interest to us," she told Randy. The other woman at the table had gone.

He glanced at Zoe, before looking at Nell. "It's of interest to me," he smiled. "I didn't get your name?"

"You're very cocky," Nell told him.

Time and again, he smiled. "I hide my insecurities."

"Only men without insecurities would joke they had any."

Randy laughed. "Unless we rely upon women thinking that," he said. "I'll look out for you tonight from Martin's Tavern." He left, without carrying a paper bag of brochures and souvenirs like the one Nell carried, becoming a little heavy in her fingers.

Passing the bag to her other hand before her fingers cramped, Nell turned back to Zoe. "I would like to come to the social tonight, Zoe," she said.

Later that afternoon, with her bag back in her accommodation and the time nearing six o'clock, Nell followed Zoe's instructions to the Women's Club social gathering. In the room were several jugs of iced tea and water on a table, along with plates of carrot pieces and a dip. Nell took a clean mug, into which she poured water.

Around her were a dozen or more women, all but one of them close to Nell's age. That one was Zoe, no longer wearing her shawl. Her blue denim jeans and blouse could have been those of any other woman there, but Nell. Hanging from Zoe's shoulder was a colorful woven bag.

A little taller than any of the women were two South-East Asian men, wearing jeans with white collarless shirts hanging loosely. They stood with a couple of women, far enough from Nell and Zoe for Nell to mention them. "Are those two men toxic?" Nell whispered to Zoe.

"That's Budi and Cipta," answered Zoe. "There are as much victims of the white male patriarchy as we are."

Nell slowly realized that all the women in the room were white. She checked other people coming to see if any of them weren't white. None were.

"Dear," said Zoe, placing her hand on Nell's arm, "you have so much to learn. I'm so glad you're here. I'll introduce you to Budi and Cipta."

Zoe led Nell to the two pale brown men. They smiled, between speaking and sipping from their mugs. Their accents were essentially American, but the region they represented weren't obvious, at least to Nell.

"Where are you from?" Nell asked them, as freshmen often asked each other. It started conversations at a university proud to host students from every American state and from many other countries, as American universities were.

"Overland Park," answered one; Nell wasn't sure if that was Budi or Cipta. "Kansas."

The other then asked Nell, "Are we the only Indonesians you've met? We're Javanese."

"I like meeting new people," nodded Nell.

They talked. Nell mingled. There could have been as many as twenty women in the room at any time; some came, others left. Budi and Cipta remained, as did Zoe and Nell.

From her colorful woven bag, Zoe removed a clear plastic sachet. Inside it were several cigarette papers and the leaves to roll in them. They weren't tobacco. "Men's rules keep us from smoking here," she told Nell, lecturing her, as Nell should expect at college, "but a quick little breather keeps me going until I can smoke safely again." Zoe opened the sachet, pulled it close to her nose, and smelt it. "Woo," she smiled, before offering it to Nell.

Nell shook her head. "I'm under twenty-one," she said.

Zoe laughed. "Fear the police," she said, "but not about this, not in Washington."

"It's bad for you."

"Don't believe the men telling you that," she told Nell, returning the sachet to her bag.

Throughout the social, Zoe moved from one conversation to another. Nell remained longer in hers.

There were no speeches, but sometime after seven o'clock, Zoe called to the dozen or so people remaining, "Excuse me, please." She gave them a moment to stop talking and face her. "You're all welcome to head up to Georgetown for a coffee with us."

A few of the women disbursed. Most of them remained with Nell and Zoe, as did Budi and Cipta. The women cleaned the room, stowing the crockery and glassware in the cupboard and food in the refrigerator to which Zoe directed them, while Budi and Cipta talked between themselves.

Carrying her colorful woven bag from her shoulder, Zoe then led the ten of them from the building to the open air, where the day was still bright; sunset wasn't due until after eight o'clock. She then led them walking to Georgetown.

The ten soon broke into smaller groups never very far apart, led by a red-headed woman who knew the way to the coffee shop Zoe had mentioned. Behind her, Nell walked with Zoe. "Couldn't we let Randy join us in the coffee shop?" asked Nell.

"Who's Randy?" asked Zoe.

"You met him when you met me this afternoon. He was the tall guy."

"Is he your boyfriend?"

"No," answered Nell, "but I like boys."

"That can change," said Zoe. "You learn something about social justice and then see who you like."

They paused at the traffic lights at an intersection, standing with the other small groups together again. "If Randy came along," persisted Nell, "I'm sure he wouldn't do anything, but talk. I'm sure he wouldn't even talk if we asked him not to."

"His presence would be aggression" explained Zoe, "and we can't have aggression. We want a time of togetherness, love, and peace."

"Without men?" asked Nell, thinking of Budi and Cipta.

"Without white men," explained Zoe.

The traffic lights changed. They all crossed the street. "I thought we believed in equality and inclusion," Nell told Zoe, as they walked.

"We do believe in equality and inclusion," insisted Zoe, "but we won't achieve real equality and inclusion until we've destroyed the source of inequality and exclusion: white masculinity."

None of it made sense to Nell. "What does your father think about that?" she asked Zoe.

"I've never met him," answered Zoe, "and I'm glad I haven't. My mother instilled in me the virtue of freeing ourselves from the shackles of men and family. I don't see her as anything but a woman: not a mother, but a woman. Don't you want to be free?"

"I feel free now."

"Oh, dear," said Zoe. "The worst oppression is that we don't even notice. You've been so conditioned, we need to release you."

The ten walked north along Wisconsin Avenue and talked, reconfiguring into different smaller groups. When Nell walked with Budi and Cipta, behind Zoe and the red-headed woman, Zoe and that woman took each other's hand.

To the left of them, nearing the intersection with N Street and well notified, appeared Martin's Tavern. As they passed, Nell could not see well enough through the glass doors and windows to identify the figures inside, before the ten of them stopped at the curb and pedestrian crossing.

A voice called from behind them: "Women's Club!"

Nell turned to see Randy at the open tavern door. He strode towards them.

"We found a spot in the tavern," he told Nell, as he reached her, before looking around at the rest of her group. "There are chairs for all of you."

"No, thank you," answered Zoe.

"I'd love to see your coffee shop," persisted Randy. "I could sit at another table until you've finished, drinking iced water."

"No," Zoe repeated.

The traffic paused and the group could have crossed the road, but Nell continued facing Randy. "What about your friends?" she asked him.

"I've told them I was looking out for you, and that if I couldn't bring you back with me, then I'd go with you. They're guys, they understand."

Zoe stepped close to Nell. "Are you starting to understand toxic masculinity?" Zoe asked her, before again facing Randy. "Won't you take 'no' for an answer?"

Nell faced him, as he faced her. His voice became gentle, as if Nell was the only person who needed to hear him. "I haven't heard 'no,' from you," he said. "I haven't heard your name, but I haven't heard 'no' from you, either."

"I'm Nell," she replied, "Nell Somersby."

Zoe turned back to the pedestrian crossing. She soon turned back to Nell.

Randy turned to Budi and Cipta, without speaking to them as much as he spoke to Zoe. His voice was again firm and loud. "You told me that men couldn't be part of the Women's Club?"

Again, Zoe stepped closer to Nell. "This is the sense of entitlement so symptomatic of the white patriarchy," she told Nell.

Randy answered. "I never much thought of myself as part of a patriarchy," he said, not obviously addressing Zoe or Nell, "on a little family ranch in an out-of-the-way part of Montana."

Nell had thought all of Montana was out of the way. She'd never been there, or anywhere near it.

Zoe stepped in front of Budi and Cipta, as if shielding them from Randy. "Don't start bullying my friends, farm boy," she told him. "They've suffered more than enough from men like you already."

"How have they suffered?" asked Randy. "They don't look like they're suffering."

"You're a student," Zoe told him. "They're not. They're friends I made today because they were visiting the campus, wanting to be students but they didn't get the grades in school and they don't have the money. How is that fair?"

"What have I done?" Randy asked her. "I've worked, earning money. I've studied, getting grades. I've not kept them from working and studying."

Zoe looked back at Nell. "If universities were serious about redressing inequality," Zoe told her, "they'd refuse admission to all the white males until all the women and people of color wanting to study were enrolled."

Randy answered her. "How is that equality?"

Zoe turned back to face him. "We must treat the unequal unequally if we're all to become equal," she lectured him.

Randy opened his arms, roaming his hands around the group before him: eight women and the two Indonesians. "Where are the women of color in your women's club?" he asked.

"They're welcome to join."

"They're with their men," Randy told her. "You're a motley cluster of white women – fine women, but still a motley cluster – thinking you represent all women."

Zoe looked at Nell. "We talk about white male aggression at Women's Club meetings," she told Nell, in the softer close-to-hand voice she reserved for Nell. "We can talk about it in the coffee shop."

The traffic behind them paused. Zoe took Nell by the arm and set off across N street. The other women walked with them, as did Budi and Cipta.

As they walked, Nell turned her head. Randy walked close behind them.

Across the street, back onto the sidewalk, Zoe turned around towards Randy. "You're harassing us," she told him, releasing Nell's arm.

"If Nell asks me to go back to the tavern, I will," he answered her.

Zoe looked at Nell. She expected an answer, and a particular answer.

Nell would disappoint her. "I can't see a problem with him sitting at another table in the coffee shop," said Nell.

"It's intrusive," answered Zoe.

"I could wait outside," said Randy, looking around at the colorful short buildings in all directions. "Georgetown is interesting. You won't know I'm there."

"We'd know," said Zoe. "For as long as you exist, thinking the way you do, we'll know and feel your power. Don't you understand?"

"I don't understand," said Randy, again looking at Zoe. "Your power doesn't bother me. Can't we deploy them together?"

Zoe stepped closer to him. "My power should bother you," she threatened him, before turning around and again walking onward. The other women walked with her, along with Budi and Cipta, but not Nell.

A few yards behind them, walking slower than they did, Nell remained with Randy. "You're from Montana," she said.

"None of my family went to college," he told her, "so it's not like I had my father's or mother's college to follow."

"Why study in Washington?"

"I wanted to spend time in our nation's capital. Some days, when I think of the country we used to be, I want to be where our founding fathers were. Other days, when I think of the country we've become, I think I'm going to head back home from my studies to Montana and spend my weekends hunting mean animals that I imagine being federal government agencies, so I should learn now what I'll be imagining later."

She smiled; Nell often smiled around Randy, but not as often as he smiled. "I don't pay attention to politics," she said, studying the old buildings they passed. "I prefer history."

Nell and Randy were falling further behind the others walking ahead. Other pedestrians became fewer along the sidewalk. Beyond the short buildings, the sun was almost setting.

"We were taught in school not to pigeonhole people," said Nell. "How did you feel about Zoe calling you 'farm boy'?"

"It's true, isn't it?" answered Randy. "I like being a farm boy; it's what I am. Whatever that says about me might be true, it might not. I don't mind there being a Women's Club and I don't mind being excluded from it, but I think it's unfair to keep white men out while letting other men in."

"Zoe should call it the Everybody-Except-White-Men's Club," said Nell. "That would be more honest."

"I wonder if she's petitioned the university to change its name to Martha Washington University," suggested Randy, looking up and around them as they walked. "We could call this Georginatown."

Sometime without realizing it, Nell had stopped looking at Zoe and her companions ahead of them. Nell stopped walking; she couldn't see them anymore. "Where are they?" she asked.

"I thought you were watching them."

Nell looked back along Wisconsin Avenue behind them. "I don't know the name of the coffee shop," she said. "I don't have Zoe's cell phone number."

Ahead of them along Wisconsin Avenue, a group of people appeared from a cross street onto the sidewalk. "Is that them?" asked Randy.

He and Nell watched the people start walking briskly towards them, not strolling contentedly as the Women's Club had strolled earlier that evening. The five or six people crossed each street as soon as they could, soon becoming recognizable as women from the Women's Club. "It is," said Nell.

She and Randy stood waiting, watching them approach. The six weren't in the smaller groups they had often been coming to Georgetown but formed a single pack. They weren't obviously talking to each other or looking around, but hurrying back along Wisconsin Avenue.

When they were close enough to Nell and Randy to hear her, without slowing or seeming to notice Nell and Randy waiting, Nell asked them, "What is it?"

"Zoe," said the red-headed woman, as the six women passed Nell.

Randy and Nell looked at each other. Zoe hadn't been among the women. It seemed that all the other women who'd come with them to Georgetown had been.

"I'll look," said Randy, hurrying forward in the direction from which the women had come.

Nell hurried with him, until they reached the spot where they'd first seen the women. Along the cross street and along Wisconsin Avenue, she couldn't see Zoe, Budi, or Cipta. A smattering of pedestrians walked calmly. With one, walked a small dog on a leash.

"You should stay here," said Randy, as he walked along the sidewalk of the cross street.

Nell didn't. She followed him.

The buildings became small homes or apartment buildings, without sign of any coffee shops or other commercial premises. At one gap between buildings, like a driveway or alleyway, Randy stopped. "Stay here," he told Nell, as he started down the darkening driveway or alleyway.

She didn't. Ahead of them, poorly lit by distant lights, Zoe stood with her back against a brick wall. Close in front of her stood Budi, his hands at her cheeks, his face at hers. Beneath him crouched Cipta, his hands under her blouse, his face at her midriff. Zoe's woven bag lay crumpled on the ground.

"Zoe," called out Randy as he hurried towards her.

She gasped. Budi pulled his hands from her cheeks and stepped backward, facing Randy.

Cipta pulled his hands from her and stood up beside Budi, also facing Randy. From under his shirt, he drew a knife he pointed at Randy.

"You'll be safer if you put that away," Randy told him, slowing as he neared them.

Nell rushed past Randy towards Zoe, who jolted back from her. Nell stopped, as Zoe rushed between Nell and the two Indonesians to the far side of the driveway or alleyway, where she held up her hands against another brick wall and hid her face between her arms.

Too close to danger, Nell rushed back to Randy, who stopped a couple of yards short of Budi, his knife still pointed at Randy, and Cipta. Randy might have been a little taller than they were, with the greater muscle that farm life required. She stepped behind and beside him, watching the two Indonesians.

Budi, his knife edging about in the air, addressed Randy. "This is nothing to do with you."

"That's not your call," replied Randy.

"There are two of us with a knife to one of you without one," said Budi, who took a cell phone from his pocket and held it close to his face. "We have friends in Washington, too."

"Invite them," said Randy. "I'll wait."

"Zoe doesn't even like you," said Budi. "She hates you. She told you to leave us. Why don't you?"

"Sometimes," said Randy, "I don't follow instructions."

Budi scoffed. "Do you think this will make her like you?"

Randy shook his head. "No," he replied.

"So you're doing this for the girl behind you," said Budi. "Do you think this will make her like you?"

Again, Randy shook his head. "No," he said. "I'm here, doing whatever I must to protect Zoe, because… it's what I do. However much she hates me and all the other white males, especially us farm boys, she's American. She'd call it white masculinity, and it probably is. There's no other reason for me to save her but patriarchy, but that's enough reason for me."

Budi and Cipta looked at each other. They then looked further along the driveway or alleyway, better lit than where they stood. Budi ran there. Cipta followed.

Nell stepped close to Zoe. "They've gone," whispered Nell, reaching her hand to Zoe's shoulder.

As Nell's hand reached her, Zoe pulled away, stepping along the wall and again burying her head in her hands against the bricks. She started to weep, as people could when danger had passed.

Remaining at a distance, Randy spoke, his voice again gentle. "We can wait until you're ready for us to walk you wherever you want to go, Zoe. Those two aren't coming back."

Zoe remained silent, but for her soft sniffling sobs slowly becoming fewer. Finally, without a word, she pulled her face from her hands and her hands from the wall. Hunched over, her blouse hanging loosely, partly open, Zoe stepped back towards the street. Randy retrieved Zoe's bag from the ground.

Nell stepped beside her. Randy stepped behind them, carrying Zoe's bag.

Without a word, in her slow-motion trek, Zoe proceeded along that street to another. She led them to an apartment building, not as nice as others but comfortable. Randy returned her bag to her.

Zoe's key struggled to unlock the building door. She looked again at it, stepped back to look up at the building face, and tried again. More carefully this time, the key unlocked the door.

Opening the door a short way, Zoe turned back towards Nell, without looking at her face but looking down. "Please," whispered Zoe, "don't tell anyone what happened tonight. The other women won't."

Nell nodded. "Yes, Zoe," she whispered.

Zoe turned back to the door, opened it enough to step inside, and did. She then started to close it, leaving Nell and Randy outside, but paused. Without looking up she whispered, "Thank you, both of you."

"I can stay with you," Nell whispered. "You might want someone with you."

Zoe closed the door. Nell waited for the chance it might open again. It didn't.

When Nell next saw her, at her home a few afternoons later, Zoe had cut her hair close to her shoulder. She wore a black blouse and slacks, sitting without a shawl.

Through the ensuing weeks, the colors of Zoe's clothes progressively became lighter. As winter neared, she began wearing skirts long enough to reach her ankles, much like Nell's winter skirts. Zoe stopped smoking, slowly leading her to realize, she told Nell, the stink it left behind in her home and clothes, before gradually abating. The Women's Club never again convened.

Amidst their lazy time together, Nell asked Randy a question she should have asked much sooner. "What led you to approach me from nowhere during Welcome Week?"

Randy looked again over her full hair and soft dress. "You're a woman who looks and acts like a woman," he told her. "I'd become tired of seeing women behaving like men, among men behaving like women."

It took some time, but Zoe became friends not just with Nell but with Randy, Nell's fiancé. Randy introduced Zoe to his father's cousin Chad, a retired Marine and widower from Wyoming, who only ever wore one kind or other of his red-checked woolen shirts. Chad was, not to put too fine a point on it, particularly masculine, but not where his children or Zoe were concerned. If Zoe ever did tell anyone what happened that night in Georgetown, before Randy and Nell arrived, she told Chad, but he never revealed anything about it.

ABOUT THE AUTHOR

Simon Lennon has lived, worked, and travelled throughout America, Europe, Australasia, Asia, and the South Pacific. He is married with six children. He is the author of the following books.

Short Story Collections
Gender in America

Novels
The King of a Vacant City
Swansong of a Childless People
A Young Man's Tale
The Insubordinate
Mahmood and Mrs Wynworth

Non-Fiction
Western Individualism
The End of Natural Selection
The Need for Nations
People's Identity
Of Whom We're Born
Biological Us
A Land to Belong
The Failure of Multiculturalism
Reclaiming Western Cultures
Christendom Lost
Aiding Islam